The People in the Photo

Hélène Gestern lives and works in Nancy. She teaches and researches in the field of linguistics at CNRS. *The People in the Photo* is her first novel.

Emily Boyce is in-house translator at Gallic Books. She lives in London.

Ros Schwartz has translated over 60 literary works. In 2009 she was made *Chevalier dans l'Ordre des Arts et des Lettres*.

The People in the Photo

The People in the Photo

Hélène Gestern

Translated from the French by Emily Boyce
and Ros Schwartz

Gallic Books
London

A Gallic Book

First published in France as *Eux sur la photo* by Éditions Arléa
Copyright © Éditions Arléa 2011

English translation copyright © Gallic Books 2014

First published in Great Britain in 2014 by
Gallic Books, 59 Ebury Street, London, SW1W 0NZ

A CIP record for this book is available from the British Library

ISBN 978-1-908313-54-6

Typeset in Fournier MT by Gallic Books
Printed and bound by CPI Group (UK) Ltd, Croydon, CR0 4YY

2 4 6 8 10 9 7 5 3 1

In memory of Madeleine Lamay

I
DARKNESS

All images will disappear
Annie Ernaux

1

The three figures in the photograph are frozen for ever, two men and a woman bathed in sunlight. All three are dressed in white and holding tennis racquets. The young woman is in the centre; the man on her right – who is quite tall – is leaning towards her as if poised to tell her something; the second man stands on her left at a slight remove, bending his knee and leaning on his racquet in a playful Charlie Chaplin pose. They all look about thirty, but the taller man is possibly a little older. The tree-covered Alpine slopes in the background are partly blotted out by a sports centre, and the snow-capped peaks on the horizon lend the scene an unreal picture-postcard feel.

This group portrait exudes carefree frivolity. Yet there is an air of seriousness about the young woman which her smile and the twinkle in her eye cannot quite disguise. She, too, is tall, less so than the man speaking to her but enough to give an impression of harmony to their appearance. Her body is slender, her beauty somewhat austere with her long face and high, round cheekbones. Her thick hair, cut short in a bob, brushes against the hollows of her cheeks. And her white hat, worn at an angle, completes her elegant look, reminiscent of the Seeberger brothers' early fashion photographs.

The man closest to her is thin, almost too thin for a man. His hair is blond (or mousey brown? It is hard to tell in black and white), wavy, cut short at the sides. The liquid limpidity of his eyes suggests the irises are blue or a very pale grey. He has a pleasant-looking face, slightly angular with sandy eyebrows, delicate features and thin lips.

The last of the trio is also the shortest. His chest, beneath a light-coloured polo shirt, is lean and sinewy; he sports a pencil moustache and a straw boater that would not have looked out of place on a dandy. Judging by the smirk on his face and his pose, he is not taking his immortalisation on film altogether seriously, as evidenced by his teasing sidelong glance at the young woman in the hat.

The picture is grainy, fuzzy on close inspection; the paper it is printed on has aged, imbuing everything with a sepia tint. The image illustrates a newspaper report on the victory of Madame N. Hivert (Ladies' Singles) and Monsieur P. Crüsten (Men's Singles) at the Interlaken Amateur Tennis Tournament, held late afternoon on 16 July 'under a clear blue sky'. The article states that the winners respectively took home a Daum *pâte de verre* cup and a writing folder. It does not, however, disclose the identity of the second man, nor explain why he is present in the photo. At the top of the clipping, a handwritten note reads 'N., Switzerland, Summer 1971'.

Ashford, 25 March 2007

Madame/Monsieur,

I have only just read your advertisement ref. 284.220 in *Libération* of 12 February.

I believe I may have some information concerning the person you are enquiring about: I am convinced it is my father, who often used to spend his summers in Interlaken. I am enclosing the photocopy of his Geneva Tennis Club membership card from the 1960s, which I have among my papers. You will see his photograph on it.

Could you tell me how you obtained his name and why you are seeking information about him?

Yours faithfully,

S. Crüsten

Madame/Monsieur,

Thank you for your letter, which I was no longer expecting. It has been over a month since I placed the advert in several French and Swiss newspapers, and the two responses I have so far received seemed fairly implausible, given the places and dates. Yours, on the other hand, leaves me in no doubt: you are the son or daughter of the 'P. Crüsten' whose name and photograph I found among my family's papers. The woman standing next to him in the picture is my mother, who passed away when I was three or four. Her married name was Nathalie Hivert (I don't know her maiden name).

My father rarely spoke of her. He died three years ago, and my adoptive mother (he remarried) has been in a nursing home for the past six months, suffering from final-stage Alzheimer's. While hunting for her medical records in my father's study, I came across an unlabelled folder containing just this newspaper clipping, which I have photocopied for you. It seems my mother and the man in the picture, your father, competed in a little tennis tournament near Interlaken and both won their categories. A local paper published an article about them and printed their names in the picture caption: it was this tiny nugget of information that prompted me to place the advert.

I know very little about my mother, and have no family to help me fill in the gaps. I am an only child and my father's two elder sisters died several years ago. I am intrigued by this photograph and would like to find out more about the people in it. Is there anything else you could tell me about your father? Do you know how he knew my mother? Is he still alive? And if so, do you think he would agree to speak to me?

I hope you don't mind me asking all these questions. Any information you could offer would mean a great deal to me.

In the meantime, thank you once again for replying to my advert.

Kind regards,

Hélène Hivert

Dear Madame Hivert,

Forgive my delay in replying to you — I am just back from a week abroad, in Johannesburg as a matter of fact, where I was attending a conference (I am a biologist).

I am delighted that my letter was helpful to you. There is no need to apologise for asking so many questions, your curiosity is perfectly understandable, and I myself am keen to find out a little more about a period of my father's life that is a mystery to me. But I'm afraid you won't be able to talk to him, since he died last year of a pulmonary embolism. So I can only give you second-hand information about his life, in the hope that it will shed some light.

My father's name was Peter Crüsten, but most of his friends called him Pierre. He was born in 1933, in Besançon, where his Swiss father had settled in the twenties and become naturalised. His mother was French. I never knew my grandfather who died quite young of a heart attack, having founded a flourishing printing works. It's still there — Crüsten Accounting

Stationery. My father studied chemistry to quite an advanced level, as well as being a musician – he was said to be a gifted pianist when he was young, but eventually he decided to become a photographer, much to my grandmother's annoyance, apparently. I know he was an army photographer during his military service, as I have seen pictures of him in the family album, posing in uniform beside his camera. After his military service, which he spent in Algeria, in conditions that were tough but could have been a lot worse, my father worked as a freelance photographer in Paris. Family legend has it that he spent some time at the Harcourt studio, but I don't have any evidence of that. He produced some impressive photos of the city in winter: the stray cats of Père-Lachaise among the frozen tombstones, the banks of the Seine covered in snow ... Then he left and set up on his own in Geneva, where some of his relatives lived. He soon became a respected photographer in his chosen field – family portraits. By the end of his life, he had several assistants working for him, trained in his 'style'; he had all but stopped taking on commissions himself.

However, he always carried on with his own work, right until the end. He was not without talent, but he never sought recognition. In Geneva we still have several hundred albums, especially landscapes and architectural complexes. One that particularly fascinates me is a series of over a hundred views of Parisian arcades, all deserted (I don't know how he miraculously persuaded the local residents to stay out of the way). His entire oeuvre is made up of beautiful, enigmatic photos in which there is hardly a single human being. My brother and I imagine he must have grown tired of photographing faces all day long.

I don't know exactly when my parents met: my grandmother told me about a dance organised in honour of the girls from the school where my mother was a boarder. A photographer was hired to record the event for posterity, and it was my father who was given the job. My mother must have liked the photo: they married in 1962, and I was born two years later. I also have a brother, Philippe, who is two years my junior. We lived in Geneva, but my grandparents owned a little chalet in Interlaken where we often used to spend our holidays.

In your advert it was the mention of that resort connected to the name Crüsten that immediately caught my eye. And, incidentally, I can tell you who the third man in the photo is: he's Jean Pamiat, a friend of my father's from his army days, who was a few years younger than him. They went through quite a lot together in Algeria, and Pierre hired him afterwards as first assistant photographer. My father asked Jean to be my godfather when I was born. I'm grateful to him, because Jean has always been like a second father to my brother and me. He is still alive and I visit him in his retirement home in Lausanne every couple of months or so. But his health has deteriorated considerably since a stroke paralysed his right side and impaired his speech.

My father was quite a solitary, taciturn man who spent most of his time in his studio, or outdoors, in search of subjects to photograph. I know little about his past. I only have a few photos of all four of us – the shoemaker's children always go barefoot! Although my mother was much younger than my father, she died in 1994 of breast cancer, and from then on he retreated into almost total silence. And so your mother's name is not familiar to me, and I don't think I ever heard him mention her.

There are several dozen boxes of photographs in the basement of our family home, which still hasn't been cleared. When I next go to Switzerland, for I now live in Kent, I will have a look through them to see if I can find any trace of those visits to Interlaken. Thanks to the newspaper clipping you kindly sent me, I now know what your mother looked like: I could leaf through the albums and try to find a photo of her.

In the meantime, I'm enclosing the photocopy – apologies for the terrible quality – of a self-portrait my father did the year he turned thirty-eight, and which used to hang in the chalet at Interlaken.

When I took it out of the frame to photocopy it, I found an inscription on the back, but I can't decipher the second part and I don't know who wrote it. In any case, I'm enclosing it as well.

This photo of my father is probably the one I like best, because he looks cheerful. In the newspaper cutting, he is wearing that same expression which we so rarely glimpsed. What a pity I can no longer ask Jean about what happened that summer of 1971.

I will of course write if I find something that might be of interest.

Kind regards,

Stéphane Crüsten

2

The man has chosen to pose in front of a large mirror so that the camera mounted on its tripod is in the frame, which also encompasses the far side of a room cluttered with a work bench, mounts and various prints. On the wall is a noticeboard pinned with snapshots, advertising postcards and two pictures of mountain peaks lost in the clouds. Despite the sheet of paper masking one side, it is also possible to make out an old photograph, probably taken from a newspaper, showing four young men in tennis whites gathered around another man wearing a black suit. A few film posters and an Art Deco-style flyer for a performance of *Véronique* at the Opéra-Comique with Paulette Merval in the title role. The man's shoulder blocks out the bottom left-hand corner of a large art print hanging midway up the wall: recognisably a Hopper, the picture shows a woman sitting alone on a bed staring straight out of the window in front of her. Despite the colours being reduced to black and white, something remains of the quiet intensity of the painting which seems to condemn its subject to brutal, eternal, stony silence.

Although there is nothing to measure him against, it feels as though the man is taller than average. He is wearing a light-coloured short-sleeved shirt and front-pleated trousers held up with a smart leather belt. No tie, though; the only thing visible around his neck is a half-moon pendant on a fine silver chain. Under the magnifying glass, however, it appears to be the top of a ring with a textured surface. His body is slim, almost thin: his collarbone shows through his shirt and the fingers of his left hand, pressed against his thigh, are slender, the swollen joints incongruous. The wedding band sits low on his ring finger as though it has slipped down a few millimetres, while his right hand is tucked casually in his pocket in an attempt to look natural, probably just after he had pressed the self-timer button.

The man stands facing the mirror in the late-morning light, which casts pale rectangles onto the wall. His hair catches the sun's rays, gleaming like an animal's pelt. Two expressive lines stripe the space between his eyebrows like inverted commas. Yet his light eyes are unblinking; the scattering of crow's feet suggests their owner is approaching forty.

Haloed by the slanting shaft of light, he looks into the mirror with a knowing expression as if his picture were being taken by a loved one and not by the lens of a Flexica. On the back, the neat inscription in French reads 'Self-portrait, studio. May 1971'. Then, in clumsy, faltering Russian, as if written by a child, are the words 'моей лисе'.

Dear Monsieur Crüsten,

Thank you for taking the time to write such a detailed response, and for the photograph. I must admit it was a bit of a shock to learn your father is no longer alive, but I was heartened to hear about your collection of old photographs. Perhaps they will tell us something. I think this could be a fruitful avenue to explore, and I'm grateful to you for opening it up to me.

Your father was a very handsome man and I can see why you like that portrait of him – he looks like a matinee idol! I should love to see some other examples of his work at some point, if possible. I confess my interest is both personal and professional: I happen to work at the Museum of the History of the Postcard as head of the pre-1930 visual artefacts collection. This means I am regularly sent collections to catalogue, sometimes from individuals (it's not unusual for them to arrive in a shoebox). Opening them up and delving into strangers' lives is definitely the most exciting part of my job; that moment of discovery gives me such a thrill, it's almost addictive. There is something very moving about the thought that just two or three sources can be enough to build a picture of an entire life.

Anyway, I digress. Although my Russian is very basic, I can just about translate the words on the back of the photo: 'For my fox'. The writer was not a Slavic speaker; you can tell by the way the letters are formed, as if they have been copied. The ink used does not quite match the inscription in French, which is a little darker, though it's hard to tell from a photocopy. I do think, however, that the lines from both alphabets were written by the same hand. Perhaps the note in Russian was simply added later? We would need to get an expert to look at it to be certain.

Did your father speak Russian or have any Russian friends? Do you know anyone to whom he might have given that nickname?

For my part, I'm pursuing my enquiries, but progress is slow. I'm frantically busy at work – I'm putting together a catalogue on the postcards of the 1900 Exposition Universelle – and haven't been able to get back to the flat to continue sorting through my parents' papers.

In the meantime, I will of course let you know if anything else comes to light.

Best wishes,

Hélène Hivert

PS My heart leapt when I saw the *Véronique* poster in the photograph. It was my stepmother's favourite operetta; she used to sing arias from it while we cooked together.

Dear Madame Hivert,

I am intrigued by the Russian inscription which you kindly translated. Intrigued and somewhat perturbed, since I find it hard to imagine my father giving my mother such a nickname. I wonder whether he might have taken that photograph, which appears to be a gift, for someone else. And of course I'm curious to know who that someone else could be. To be frank, your letter has reawakened an old sense of unease and suspicion; for a very long time I have been wondering what really went on in my parents' lives.

To return to the subject, as far as I know, my father did not have any Russian friends, but I know that Jean Pamiat spoke the language fluently (where had he learned it?), and had connections with several St Petersburg families. He called my father *tovarish* (I'm not sure of the spelling), as a joke, and actually it took me ages to realise that it wasn't a first name, like Igor or Sasha.

I also went with my father, once, towards the end of his life, to the Russian Orthodox section of Thiais cemetery. He was already very frail, but he insisted that I take him there. I don't know which grave he visited, because he asked me to wait for him at a distance. Nor do I know the reasons for this pilgrimage. It is a tenuous clue, but it confirms that there could have been a Russian link. That seems to be where this trail is leading us.

Let's keep each other posted.

Kind regards,

Stéphane C.

Paris, 6 June 2007

Dear Monsieur Crüsten,

I'm sorry if what I have told you makes you uncomfortable. If you would rather not carry on, we can stop now. But I won't deny it would be a blow to me; now that I've made the decision to find out, I want to follow it through. I have spent my whole life surrounded by so much silence, trying to tell myself it didn't matter, but as time goes on the unanswered questions gnaw away at me. I want to find out more about my mother's life; I know almost nothing about her. Yet at the same time I'm aware that digging up the past is risky. Who knows what secrets they were trying to protect us from and at what cost?

It's not too late to put a stop to this. I could always continue on my own if you're concerned about where it might lead. Let me know your thoughts.

Kind regards,

Hélène H.

Dear Madame Hivert,

For once I'm replying to you by email. I very much enjoy receiving letters from you and writing to you (the quaint delights of corresponding), but at the moment I'm in Florida, and I didn't want to delay my answer any longer.

I fear that my last letter may have given rise to a misunderstanding, by suggesting that I had misgivings about our investigation. As I said to you in one of my earlier letters, one of the reasons that prompted me to write to you is that my father remains largely a mystery to my brother and myself. He was a fairly distant, solitary, silent man. It was almost impossible to have a conversation with him. When we were children, he found our boisterousness irritating, and would often leave the table in the middle of a meal. He'd come home several hours later, and we had no idea where he had been. And yet, I have memories of him dating back to an earlier time when he was more cheerful: I recall in particular when he taught me to ride a bicycle and to tell the time, on a big light-blue alarm clock bought specially for the purpose (probably some Swiss throwback!). He started teaching me to play tennis, and I remember sunny afternoons spent on the club terrace with Jean Pamiat. He sometimes came with a friend, Friedrich, whose sunglasses and leather jacket fascinated me.

I don't know exactly when my father's behaviour changed. I thought it was to do with a marital row. My mother, Anna Krüger, was the daughter of a bourgeois family from Lausanne, a dynasty of bankers and insurance brokers, and I know that her parents had been very much against her marrying my father. It seems they were swayed by their daughter's determination. I even heard on occasion, during a family meal, my maternal grandfather refer to Pierre as 'the Gypsy', which made Philippe and me very curious: we couldn't understand what our father had to do with those people we'd seen in films who lived in caravans and played the fiddle in the street!

Meanwhile, my grandmother Crüsten, a resourceful woman who had taken over the printing works after her husband's death, was not well disposed towards her daughter-in-law. She would always make fun of the Swiss, saying they had swallowed a cuckoo. I believe her sniping concealed a deeper grievance: my mother relished being a housewife, and was even proud of it. She always refused to work, even in the early years when the studio barely brought in any money. My grandmother, who had fought in the Resistance, been a political activist and struggled to keep a business going, found my mother's dependence irksome.

During our summer stays in Besançon, she would wake us up at seven every morning and give us all chores to do in the printing works, trumpeting, 'Roll your sleeves up, the petty bourgeoisie!' but we were very fond of her. She was a delightful woman, brave and funny; she had taken huge risks during the war, printing false documents for families in the area. She loved telling us how she had made a false ration card for a neighbour, a Pole whom she hated because he used to hit his cats 'but we couldn't let the man die of starvation'. She got her own back by printing his surname as Dumkopfsky.

Forgive me, I'm straying off the subject, but I was very fond of my grandmother and like reminiscing about her. We visited her less often in the latter years of her life – she and my father fell out, I think – and that saddens me.

Going back to my mother, she was a sweet person, but with strong principles, who devoted her life to her husband and raising her children. At one point, I don't know why, there were explosive rows in our family. These were followed by days, weeks even, when my parents refused to speak to each other. They argued in the evening, after we'd gone to bed: they must have thought that the partitioning would stifle the noise. I didn't understand what they were arguing about, but I was always amazed to hear my mother, a model of placidity and restraint, raise her voice. As for Philippe, he would start crying and crawl into my bed seeking comfort.

My father got into the habit of spending the night in his studio where he had installed a divan, a tiny bathroom and a gas ring. He rarely slept at home, returning only when my mother began her chemotherapy. But as far as I know, he did not have any affairs; in any case, I didn't see or hear anything that ever made me think he did. On the contrary, he sank further and further into extreme solitude and silence. He spoke only in monosyllables or to give curt instructions. If it hadn't been for his assistants, who dealt with the customers, I think he'd have had to shut up shop. After the breakdown of their marriage, which was the year Philippe had his bicycle accident – in 1973 if I'm not mistaken – my parents became distant, and remained so. My brother and I are convinced that there must have been one or several serious events that were kept secret from us, but we never dared ask any questions. While we were at school, my mother spent a lot of time at the Lutheran church and found some sort of comfort there, I think, and she had her charity work. My father was often away. Once or twice, he took me with him on his photographic expeditions, but I was too little to be of much use, not able to operate the equipment fast enough. We did not repeat the experience. The result was that we were hardly a close family. My parents did not eat together, except when we had visitors. And I remember entire days spent in a leaden silence. Philippe and I sometimes whispered all day long in order not to disturb the atmosphere, which was poisonous in the extreme. To be honest, my parents were so unhappy together that I find it hard to understand why they didn't divorce. True, my mother had no resources, but her parents, the Krügers, were wealthy enough to provide for her. On the other hand, in the seventies, the stigma of divorce in middle-class circles made people accept unpalatable arrangements.

You tell me that for a while you refused to acknowledge the importance of those family silences. For a long time, I tried to convince my brother (who was very upset by the situation) to adopt the same attitude, telling him – telling myself above all – that raking over the past wouldn't change it and that we should turn the page. I would be less dogmatic today. You and I are strangers, but we know each other well enough, given the circumstances that have brought us together, for me to be able to tell you that I am unmarried and do not have any children. This deliberate decision has a lot to do with the sight of my unhappy parents, a situation that I had no wish to replicate. I'm now older than the age my father was at the time we are talking about. I'd like to understand what happened to make him walk out on us. I too feel that inner emptiness, which you describe so poignantly. And, as I grow older, I find it increasingly hard to bear. The fact is, I do not know the man who fathered me.

I hope you'll forgive me this rambling email, and

for sharing these family secrets, which you might find inappropriate since we have never even met.

I have not spoken about this to anyone for years, and I fear I may have let myself go. Let us say that this quest is as important to me as it is to you; take these words as proof that my desire to uncover the missing portion of my past is as strong as yours.

It will be night time in Paris when you receive this message.

Kind regards,

Stéphane

Paris, 16 June (email)

Thank you for being so open with me, Stéphane. It means a lot. Let's keep going then. Letter to follow very soon.

Warm wishes,

Hélène

Miami, 18 June 2007 (postcard)

Dear Hélène,

Greetings from Florida, where the beaches are as beautiful as in the photograph, even though the conference doesn't leave me much time to enjoy them.

I'll write soon.

Stéphane C.

3

The passport-sized photo, which the scissors have not cut quite square, is affixed to the pink card by two brass eyelets, one in the bottom left-hand corner and the other in the top right. The subject wears an unsmiling, almost sullen expression. Her mane of shoulder-length hair is tamed as far as possible by two metal slides at the temples, their gleam picked out by the flash. Her dark eyes are wide-open as if dazzled by the light, her brow is furrowed and her full lips form a pout. But her chin is softened by a dimple which punctuates the perfect oval of her face. Her forehead appears slightly domed – distorted, no doubt, by the camera angle. The paleness of her skin contrasts with the murky grey background, while her striped blouse brings an element of geometry to the composition and reveals a glimpse of long, white neck wearing a fine chain.

The document was issued at the Paris prefecture on 14 March 1959 by a Monsieur Félix Thoiry on behalf of the prefect. The driving licence relates to category B automotive vehicles. At the bottom of the rectangle, neatly signed in heavy ink, is a square monogram with the initials N and Z intertwined.

Above the photograph, it is written that the bearer of this driving licence is called Zabvina, Nataliya Olegovna, that she was born on 4 January 1941 in Archangelsk (USSR) and that her place of residence is 142 Rue de la Mouzaïa, Paris (19th *arrondissement*).

Paris, 25 June 2007

Dear Stéphane,

I hope you got back from Florida safely and that you managed to catch at least a few rays of sunshine while you were there.

I'm sorry it has taken me so long to write to you as promised. Getting the catalogue on the Exposition Universelle done turned out to be no mean feat and I haven't had much time to make any further enquiries.

I wanted to let you know how much it meant to me to get your long email: you cannot imagine how strongly your account of a broken family chimes with me, in spite of our very different circumstances. Yes, it is unbearable not knowing. Our families' silence is a poison that infects everything it touches: our dreams, our fears, our entire adult lives. And it leaves us with nothing but questions to fall back on, thirty or forty years down the line (I don't think I told you my age: I'm thirty-eight).

I didn't get a chance to go to my parents' flat until last weekend. This time, I decided to trawl through everything methodically, opening up each file and folder one by one. Given the volume of papers and the very little spare time I have at present, I expect it will take me several weeks to get through it, but I'm fairly certain the answer is in there somewhere and I'm determined not to miss anything. I have to say, though, I felt very uneasy about rifling through my parents' things; it's as though I'm raiding their lives. Sad, too, because the study reminds me of my father and I miss him. As I write, I can still smell the scent of his tobacco and his favourite old leather armchair, where I sit and read sometimes when I'm over there.

By five o'clock, I was ready to call it a day, having drawn a blank. I was straightening up a row of hardbacks on one of the top bookshelves (a pet obsession of mine), when I met some resistance. I fetched the stepladder, took down the books and discovered a notebook that had dropped behind them. It turned out to be a log-book kept by my father, who was in the medical corps, in which he recorded details of some of his tours of duty off New Caledonia and the West Indies between 1968 and 1974. There was nothing much in it besides weather reports, daily menus and route maps, accompanied by sketches of plants and nautical charts. But tucked inside the cover, I came across a document I wasn't expecting: my mother's driving licence. From it, I learned that my mother's maiden name was Nataliya Olegovna Zabvina and that she was born on 4 January 1941 in 'Archangelsk' (the official must have copied it down wrong). There was also an address in Rue de la Mouzaïa in Paris.

Needless to say, I was astonished. Evidently my mother was Russian and had lived in Paris in her youth. I knew none of this, of course, because it was my adoptive mother Sylvia's name that was on my birth certificate. I don't understand why my roots have been hidden from me, or why I've been told so many lies. This discovery has left me shaken, to say the least.

The irony is that fate chose to inform me of this through a driving licence, when I've never managed to pass my test even after four attempts, one of which has gone down in the annals of my driving school (I fainted at the wheel and almost got us killed).

You told me you found it difficult to come to terms with your background. As for me, I've been plagued by anxiety my whole life. My mind is filled with images I can't explain, scenes of catastrophe and things falling apart. I have rarely been able to shake this sense of anguish, even at what should have been the happiest times of my life. This probably explains why I have found it so hard to build anything lasting; I never wanted children either, for the same reasons as you, I think.

None of this is really so terrible in itself. Yet the familiar, invisible burden becomes harder to bear with every year that passes. I'm a chronic asthma sufferer, which I now put down to the suffocating weight of silence. There's something neat about this psychosomatic explanation, but above all it allows me to give form to the crushing emptiness of my memory.

In any case, every time I have an asthma attack, I'm relieved that no one will inherit this from me.

I intend to visit my mother's old address, which is somewhere near the Buttes-Chaumont. But for the time being, I think I need to step back and mull it all over.

All the best,

Hélène

Ashford, 28 June (email)

Dear Hélène,

I can't put myself in your shoes, but I imagine you must be reeling. When you said you knew little of your mother's life, I didn't realise you were ignorant even of her nationality and date of birth. I don't know what could have made your parents conceal all that from you, but, looking back, such secrecy seems extremely cruel. This time, I'm the one who fears I'm prying, but what exactly were you told about your mother, and how did she die? Do you have any other documents besides that driving licence? I'd like to go to Geneva as soon as possible to look through the albums, but I'm stuck in my laboratory working on an experiment that's going to require at least a month and a half of daily observations (no rest for scientists). Do you think you can wait until August? In the meantime, let me give you my phone number here in England. It's at the bottom of this email in the signature. If you'd like to talk about all this over the phone, don't hesitate to call me.

All the best,

Stéphane

Paris, 1 July (email)

Dear Stéphane,

Just a note to thank you for your offer and comforting words. For the time being, I think I need some space to reflect on what I've found out, but I'll give you a call soon. It will be nice to hear your voice.

Best wishes,

Hélène

Ashford, 8 July (email)

Dear Hélène,

Thank you for your phone call the other evening. It was a pleasure to be able to talk to you in person at last. That said, I very much enjoy writing and receiving letters, and sometimes I watch out for the postman. So I hope that as well as talking to each other, we will continue to write.

All the best,

Stéphane

Paris, 11 July 2007

Dear Stéphane,

Now that my mini existential crisis has blown over, I'm ready to pick up my pen again. By the way, I forgot to ask the other day: what is this experiment that's keeping you in England?

You ask how much I know about my mother. The answer is simple: nothing. Let me tell you something. When I found that newspaper clipping, and particularly when I read the caption at the bottom, it literally took my breath away because it was the first time I had actually *seen* my mother's face. And not only that, I had to *deduce* that it was her from the name below the photo – without it, I would never have recognised her. Of course I must have seen that face hundreds of times as a child, but my memory of it has vanished. Growing up, I was never shown any pictures of Nathalie (as my father called her, on the two or three occasions he referred to her), no matter how many times I asked. My father and Sylvia always told me that the album had been lost when they moved house(!). When I asked them what my mother looked like, he would reply that she was beautiful and then he'd change the subject. Even as a teenager, I thought nothing of the fact that *no one* had kept a single portrait of her, not even a passport photo.

My whole childhood, I never knew how my mother had died. I remember a period of a few months, when I was eight or nine, when I constantly pestered the grown-ups about it. One day, when I had been asking the same thing over and over at the dinner table in that way children have of repeating things and no doubt driving their parents to distraction ('But how did Nathalie die?'), my father, who'd stayed silent throughout, stood up and calmly slapped my face, twice: 'That's enough.' Then he went back to his omelette. That was the only time in his life he ever raised a hand to me and it was such a shock that I didn't even cry. Needless to say, I never broached the subject with him again.

Later on, as a teenager, I grilled Sylvia but she remained tight-lipped. She had this way of avoiding my gaze and dodging the question which made it obvious from the start that I wasn't going to get anything out of her. When I pressed her on the whereabouts of my mother's grave, she reluctantly told me that she had been cremated and her ashes scattered off the coast of Brittany.

It was one of my aunts who let the cat out of the bag at my eighteenth birthday dinner. After the meal (during which she'd had rather a lot to drink), she came into the kitchen for a cigarette while I was making coffee. She asked me what I would like as a gift to mark my coming of age. I replied: tell me how my mother died. I remember that moment very clearly: the sudden silence amid all the noise, the loud gurgling of the coffee machine on one side, the regular whiffs of pungent smoke on the other. I didn't dare turn round. I heard my aunt's voice say in a strange tone: 'Your mother died in a car accident. She veered off the road in bad weather and flipped over into a ravine.' Just then, as if he had sensed danger, my father came into the kitchen and eyed us both with suspicion. My aunt said nothing more and went back out into the garden. When I brought it up again the next time I saw her, her expression hardened and she said she had been wrong to say anything, that I should forget all about it and concentrate on the future. Forget about what? How could I forget what I had never known?

I was nine when my father married Sylvia. By then, we had been seeing her almost every week for several years. My father never told me how he met her, but I can remember her coming on holiday with us before she moved into our apartment on Rue de l'Observatoire in Paris. She was always wonderful with me, very gentle; it wasn't long before I asked if I could call her 'Maman', I was so fond of her. She was incredibly accomplished and well-read, and always looked stunning, even well into her old age. A woman of impeccable taste with a wonderful turn of phrase, but not the slightest bit aloof: she was warm and sociable and loved entertaining. She was a librarian and then became head curator of the manuscripts department at the Bibliothèque Nationale. Although it was against the rules, I remember her taking me into the Labrouste reading room as a small child. I was so overwhelmed by the sight of so many books, I thought they must have been painted on the walls.

Life at home was much more fun with her around. Before then, my father had moved house frequently: I still have photographs of a town whose name I don't remember, and pictures taken in Polynesia where we lived for several months. In one of them, I'm sitting on the lap of a large mixed-race woman with frizzy hair, probably my nanny. I've forgotten everything about the people I met and the houses I lived in, but never the hours I spent at school worrying whether my toys and stuffed cat would still be there when I got home. I'm told I used to have nightmares every night.

In Paris, Sylvia cared for me as her own child: she came to pick me up, gave me cuddles, made my tea and told me bedtime stories. I was overjoyed to have a mother at last. I had forgotten my own mother – I'm still unable to summon a single memory of her, no matter how hard I try – and above all, I was sick of the constant moves, the playground whispering and pitying glances. I think I even stopped speaking for a while; at least, I can picture my father growing angry in the attempt to get a sound out of me.

Sylvia and my father would have liked to have children

of their own. In a very right-on, typically eighties way, they sat me down in the kitchen one afternoon and asked if it would make me happy to have a little brother or sister. It's funny to think of it now. Not least because I would have loved it. But I think there was a miscarriage and after that they stopped trying. In any case Sylvia, who had legally adopted me a year after their marriage, lavished all her love on me. I owe her such a lot, right down to the career she inspired me to follow. She made my father happy, as far as she could — he was never the easiest person to get along with. They grew old together, more or less gracefully, and it was after he passed away three years ago that her illness was diagnosed.

I have been going to see her three times a week since she went into a home, but she has forgotten who I am. Sometimes she gabbles non-stop like a radio, other times she says nothing for several days. She can no longer dress or feed herself or walk unaided. As she is also suffering from emphysema, the doctors say she doesn't have long left. I hadn't paid much attention to it before now, but I have been surprised a few times over the last couple of months to hear her come out with snatches of Russian. And yet I never heard her speak a word of Russian in all the years she lived with us. I shall try to listen more closely from now on to see if I can pick out any words or names.

Meanwhile, there's a certain irony in the fact that our progress depends on the shaky recollections of a man whose brain is half-dead and an old lady with a ravaged memory. A curious allegory for the present we're piecing back together, one photo at a time.

Best wishes,

Hélène

Dear Hélène,

Yes, here we are playing the family archaeologists, and this situation isn't exactly comfortable, even though we sometimes get caught up in the game. From time to time I tell myself that if we draw a blank, at least I'll have had the opportunity of getting to know you and sharing with you some of the silences that weigh so heavily on me ordinarily. But reading your letter, I realise the silences you have had to deal with are much worse than mine. Even if your adoptive mother was loving, it must have been difficult to grow up knowing nothing of the person who brought you into the world.

You ask about the experiment that is keeping me in England. I am trying to isolate the genetic markers that make it possible to identify the links between certain species of trees. You could say I am an expert on tree DNA! That makes people laugh when I talk about my work in a social situation, and I'm nicknamed the CSI of the plane tree (I'm barely exaggerating), but you have no idea how much plant life has to teach us about the workings — and above all the malfunctions — of human life.

I have been researching the subject for over twenty-five years, but I feel as though I'm only at the beginning of a study that could take several lifetimes. At home, I also have a garden, hence my choice to live outside London. I have fun in it growing a few rare specimens. No need to tell you that the results sometimes astonish the neighbours.

I'm thinking of going to Geneva around 20 August. My suggestion might sound a little inappropriate, but I was wondering whether you would like to come too and sort through the photographs with me. Who better than you to recognise your mother and other people in the photos? And I also thought that being an archivist you'd enjoy discovering my father's work, his cityscapes, in particular. We could also take the opportunity to drop in and say hello to Jean Pamiat on the way back: I'm sure he'd be delighted to see you, if he knew your mother well. The house is big and has a private guest apartment: so no problem on that front. But perhaps you have other holiday plans, or someone special keeping you in Paris? In any case, feel free to accept or refuse my invitation.

I hope to hear from you very soon.

Warmest wishes,
Stéphane

Dear Stéphane,

Thank you for your invitation, which I would be delighted to accept. Sylvia no longer has any sense of time and I now realise it makes little difference to her whether she goes forty-eight hours or three weeks without seeing me. It's awful, but that's the way it is. In reality, the only significant other keeping me in Paris is my cat, Bourbaki. I'll leave him with my neighbour, who adores him and spoils him outrageously.

What's more, it means I will finally have the pleasure of meeting you 'in real life'. It seems rather old-fashioned nowadays, but I always enjoy actually meeting people I have corresponded with in the flesh, especially once they've become friends.

Yesterday I went to Rue de la Mouzaïa to visit the address on the driving licence. I found number 142 and rang the doorbell, but the shutters were closed and there was no answer. The owners must be away; I will try again once the holidays are over.

Nevertheless, it was strange to think I was taking the same route my mother must have walked every day, and as I passed through the *quartier* (which is really rather lovely, by the way) I tried to see it as she would have done, as the backdrop to her daily life. Did she ride her bike or play ball on the pavement? Did she sit by the window watching visitors arrive? As I put my hand to the doorknob, it occurred to me that hers must have turned that same knob dozens of times, and it was as though all these years later we were somehow able to touch one another across time. I came home feeling very shaken and quite melancholy.

Because of this, I've decided to take another break from my enquiries, which are turning out to be more emotionally draining than I had envisaged, and am heading to Deauville for a few days (with Bourbaki). Let's speak when I get back to sort out the details of our Geneva trip. I'm really looking forward to going through the photos with you.

Best wishes,

Hélène

4

The photograph is creased, its edges dog-eared. A thick stripe, where it has been folded, cuts vertically down the centre of the image. It shows a group of children and teenagers of varying ages, flanked by three adults: a bearded man in vestments and two women of average build. There are about fifteen people in the picture altogether and none of them is smiling. Behind them, a painted wooden panel that appears to be a screen is just visible; the presence, to its left, of an Orthodox cross tells us it is in fact an iconostasis and that the photo was taken inside a church.

The hairstyles, the shape of the glasses and cut of the clothes suggest the picture dates from the 1950s. From the slightly dishevelled appearance of the youngest boys, the dusty shoes, tartan skirts and coarse cloth smocks, it is apparent that all or most of the subjects are working-class. Standing a little apart to the right, a very fair-haired adolescent girl marks herself out from the group both in stance and facial expression — that of a princess who has strayed among paupers. She wears her glossy hair in a thick braid drawn back so tightly at the temples that they reflect the light from the flash. She has on a plain, light-coloured dress with a slightly low-cut neckline, the hem falling just below the knee, worn with ankle boots and a neck scarf. A small bag hangs demurely from her forearm. Her blasé expression and slightly aloof air, like a film star weary of being hounded by paparazzi, are probably modelled on a cover girl.

Next to her, a girl of about the same age – fifteen or so – stands tall, thin and rather gawky in an oversized man's raincoat and strap shoes. Her thick, slightly wavy hair is tied back but several strands have escaped to fall around her face. Her high cheekbones and slightly slanting eyes would give her an Asian or Slavic appearance if the butterfly-frame glasses had not imposed their Western geometry on her exotic features. She has her hands in her pockets, her white socks are rucked and her angular bone structure gives her a tomboy look. To her left is a short young man with the ghost of a moustache. He must have borrowed his suit jacket and loosely knotted tie from his father. He has slicked his hair back, but a sweet little curl has flopped back onto his forehead. Puffing out his chest, he looks every bit the romantic male lead, or like a teenage Marcel Proust.

On the back of the photo, someone has written in French, 'Saint-Serge parish choir, La Mouzaïa, 1955'.

Deauville, 1 August 2007 (postcard)

Dear Stéphane,

Greetings from Deauville, where the beach is even more perfect than it looks in the photo. I hope all's well with your trees' DNA, and with you too.

All the best,

Hélène

Dear Hélène,

Thank you for your card. Did Bourbaki go swimming? I've finally made my plans for the journey: since I was able to get a reasonably priced ticket on the Shuttle, I'm going to drive to Geneva. So I could come via Paris and pick you up: we just need to agree on the day, the time and the place.

Phone me this evening if you like, to finalise arrangements.

Warmest wishes,

Stéphane

PS One of my plane trees has just been cleared thanks to its genetic fingerprint. I'm seeking another culprit.

Dear Stéphane,

I took advantage of my time off to go back to Rue de l'Observatoire and do a bit more sorting before we leave. While I was there I came across something which I have scanned and wanted to send you straight away.

My father, who was an old-fashioned scholar, amassed a collection of specialist dictionaries over his lifetime, particularly botanical ones, and he spent a good part of his retirement poring over them, pencil in hand. When Sylvia was still more or less *compos mentis*, she asked me to catalogue them and to hold on to a couple of volumes as a reminder of him.

I started dusting them off yesterday, hoping to come across some rare botanical tome that might be of interest to you. Instead I spotted an odd one out, an old Makarov Russian–French dictionary. It was so tatty that it almost fell apart in my hands when I took it down from the shelf. As I was trying to slot the loose sheets back in, I noticed a slight bulge between the centre pages: something had been slipped inside. I opened it up and found what I initially took to be a class picture, but in fact it's a photo of a choir.

There are no names written on it, which is a real shame. But I would say the young woman with her hands in her pockets could well be my mother. She looks like a much younger version of the woman in the newspaper clipping, only with a different haircut. It's something about her expression. What do you think? And what's more, I would swear blind the rather uptight-looking blonde girl is my adoptive mother, Sylvia. I recognise her eyes, the look on her face and the slightly rigid posture, like that of a ballet dancer. And I'm absolutely amazed to see her there. As a teenager, when I asked her about my mother, she always claimed never to have met her. Yet they must be about fifteen in this picture, which means they were actually childhood friends. The web of lies is even more complex than I imagined. What exactly they're hiding is still a mystery.

I doubt Sylvia will be able to enlighten me, as her illness is in its advanced stages. She doesn't know who I am any more. But I've been told that Alzheimer's sufferers sometimes have clear long-term recollections. I will try to talk to her about it, if I catch her on a day when I can get through to her – mostly she's in her own little world. Several times over the last few months she has called me 'Natasha', which I had put down to her simply muddling names. But if that really is my mother in the photo, Sylvia must be taking me for the girl she used to see at the Orthodox church as a teenager.

The inscription on the back gives the same road name as the driving licence. I had a look online and it seems there is still an Orthodox church in the area called Saint-

Serge de Radonège. I'll head over there and take a look before we go, and will let you know what I find out.

See you very soon!

Hélène

Dear Hélène,

I've looked closely at the photo you sent me. Like you, I'm almost certain that the brunette is the same woman as the one in the newspaper cutting. And I have another clue: I believe that the young man dressed like a dandy is Jean Pamiat. His face looks familiar. I'm not absolutely sure, but it would fit with his appearance and his style, and would perhaps explain how our parents met. If your mother, Nathalie, and he were childhood friends and kept in touch as adults, he would certainly have introduced her to his closest friend, my father, at some point. We'll be seeing Jean in a few days. As I believe I've already told you, he is very frail, it's almost impossible to understand what he is saying, and I don't know whether he is able to remember anything. But we communicate, a little, through exclamations and hand signs, and if I move my finger slowly over the alphabet, he is able to 'dictate' little messages by blinking. We'll talk to him about Nataliya Zabvina and perhaps that will stimulate his memory.

In the meantime, I'm busy preparing for our trip, and

I too am looking forward to it. I love my trees, but at the moment they are a hindrance. I expect to arrive in Paris on the evening of the 24th, and I've made a note of how to get to our meeting place. I have taken the liberty of booking a table at the Épicerie Russe, in Rue Daru – it seemed an appropriate place to celebrate our meeting! Even if the reasons that made us turn detective are no laughing matter, I must confess I'm getting caught up in this adventure and can imagine several scenarios, and events – it's like putting together a jigsaw puzzle. I probably watch too much TV.

See you very soon.

Stéphane

24 August (text message)

Left five voicemails after you'd set off, but don't know if you've picked them up. Hospital rang: Sylvia has pneumonia again and is in a very bad way. Can't come to Geneva. Will send news when I can. Hélène.

24 August (text message)

I'm so sorry. You are very much in my thoughts. All the best. Stéphane

24 August (text message)

Sylvia in critical condition, prognosis not good. Must stay with her. Drive carefully. H.

24 August (text message)

Be strong. Thinking of you. Stéphane

5

The photo was taken outdoors under an arbour, at the end of a meal: a Sunday lunch or special occasion, judging by the fine china and white tablecloth. There are five people sitting at a round table on which all that remains apart from a few napkins, a sugar bowl, teaspoons and wine glasses, one of which is half full, is a copper samovar surrounded by little tea bowls. On the left of the image sits a matronly woman in a black dress, the bottom half of which is partly covered by a paler fabric, most likely an apron. The photographer must have told her to turn her chair in and sit at a slight angle so that he could see her face. She has black hair with white streaks, parted neatly in the middle, almond eyes and high cheekbones flushed from the sun, or from the wine. Her features are softened by plumpness but the bone structure of her face is still firm, and there is a little beauty spot above her top lip. Her hands are neatly folded in her lap. A fat black and white cat lies stretched out at her feet, eyes closed, relishing the coolness of the flagstones against its thick fur.

Next to the woman is an empty place where the

photographer must have been sitting. In the next chair is Jean Pamiat, dapper as always in a blazer and straw boater, wearing a bow tie and a pale shirt. The waxed tips of his pencil moustache are turned up at the ends, lending him the same old-fashioned air he has in almost every picture. To his left, Nataliya Zabvina is also wearing a hat, a wide-brimmed one that casts a shadow over part of her forehead. She looks straight at the camera, myopic eyes wide open, smiling in amusement at something. Her hands are placed in front of her on the table. One hand, displaying a finely engraved silver ring on the fourth finger, is holding an unlit cigarette. The other is closed around something, probably a lighter. Next to Nataliya, a young man with a crew cut sits awkwardly in a suit and striped tie. He is unsmiling and seems uncomfortable in front of the camera which has captured him with his mouth part open, giving an impression of gormlessness.

The last person in frame should be sitting next to this young man, but has moved to avoid having his back to the camera, which is perhaps why he is standing behind Nataliya; he seems to have chosen not to sit in the photographer's place. He is blond, clean-shaven, his hair shorn in an almost regulation cut. His dark glasses sit on top of his head. He too holds a cigarette, but a lit one with a thin curl of smoke rising from it. His other hand, out of sight, is probably resting on the back of Nataliya's chair. The man is tall, dressed in smart, crisp front-pleated trousers, a light-coloured short-sleeved shirt and a plain tie. His relaxed pose, bronzed skin, glasses and slight smile at the camera in no way detract from his elegant bearing.

The wall behind them is partly covered with ivy, but a door can be glimpsed. Its lintel is decorated with ceramic tiles in the style of an Etruscan mosaic, overgrown in places by dense vegetation. The wisteria flowering under the arbour has wound itself around the frame and its lush foliage suggests the photo was taken in late spring or early summer. All the lunch guests, with the exception of the young man on the right of the picture, have the satiated, slightly hazy look that comes from eating well, no doubt accentuated by the warmth of the sun. And at the centre of the picture, Nataliya and Pierre, eternally joined by chance – places at a table, a hand resting on a chair, some gelatin and a dash of silver nitrate – look like lovers betrothed for evermore.

Dearest Hélène,

I'm glad to hear that Sylvia is recovering and has regained consciousness, even if the prognosis is not very reassuring. I hope I didn't bother you too much when I called the hospital last night. I was concerned about you.

Don't worry about Geneva. Let's just say it's postponed and we'll find another opportunity. We'll make one, if need be.

My task here is turning out to be more difficult than I anticipated. My father left more than a hundred boxes, each one containing several albums, but they were packed up any old how by the removal men who cleared out his studio. Result: although the albums are all dated, I still haven't managed to pick up the trail, since the years are all muddled up. At first, I selected boxes at random. As I opened each one, I hoped for a miraculous find, but soon realised that this frantic activity wouldn't get me anywhere. So now I'm going through the boxes one at a time, as you are doing in your parents' apartment, and I'm trying to put them in chronological order. Each box weighs a ton, making the job all the more difficult. Over the last few days, the only area in which I've made any progress is in the aches and pains department!

Being back in Geneva is quite strange. Not all my memories of this bland and deceptively sleepy city are happy. Returning to my parents' former home has stirred other recollections that are no more positive. My self-imposed exile in England is probably a means of escaping both from the place and the past associated with it. Sometimes, when I think I might have lived and worked here, I'm glad I found the courage to leave.

I hope all's well with you, despite your current worries.

All the best,

Stéphane

PS Eureka! I'm opening the letter up again because I almost misled you: flicking through an album from 1960 (views of Paris) before going to bed, I've just found a photo which I think will greatly interest you. I'll photocopy it tomorrow and pop it into the envelope. I'm very excited about it actually: this time, we have the link between our parents. Do you recognise this little garden or courtyard?

Dear Stéphane,

I've just received your letter from Switzerland, with the photocopy of the picture. Looking at it has made me emotional, almost overwhelmingly so. Your father and my mother look so young, so beautiful and – there's no denying it – so perfectly matched. I feel I am looking at a picture of a couple. This leads me to a rather delicate question I have been mulling over for some time, but which you may find a shocking suggestion: do you think our parents might once have had a relationship? A love affair, I mean? You told me Jean Pamiat met your father during their military service. Let's say Jean made the most of a few days' leave to take his pal to Paris for lunch with an old friend from church, and Pierre fell in love with Nataliya? Or maybe it was Jean who was in love with Nataliya, and your father simply kept the photo as a reminder of Sunday lunch with one of his army buddies?

I could well be barking up the wrong tree altogether and reading far too much into these pictures, of course. But we can safely say that our parents knew each other well before Interlaken, and well before their respective marriages too. What I don't know is where the picture might have been taken; I don't recognise the place at all.

I'm also puzzled by the other people sitting around that table. Studying the photo more closely, it seems to me that the stout woman on the left and Nataliya resemble one another: look at the Slavic cheekbones and eyes. I wonder if I might be looking at a picture of my maternal grandmother for the first time, the grandma I never knew. And that thought has just made me cry. I suppose my present emotional state may have something to do with it.

I really hope all this speculation doesn't upset you, although I don't think either of us would judge our parents – it's not our place to judge them, no matter what they may have done. And I would like to talk to you about it face to face. Sylvia's condition seems to have stabilised, for the time being at least, so I have a suggestion: when you come through Paris on your way back from Geneva, how about dropping in for a coffee or dinner at my place? It would be a good chance for us finally to meet and discuss some of these questions.

Warmest wishes,

Hélène

Geneva, 30 August (email)

Dear Hélène,

Thanks to my 3G dongle, I've just picked up your email and am replying straight away.

I'm so sorry the photo upset you. No wonder, I can imagine how distressing it must be to discover the existence of a family you have never known.

I appreciate your concern, but you don't need to worry about my reaction to suppositions that I have shared from the start. Like you, I think that there was something between our parents: I'm convinced they had an affair, and that it was definitely to Nataliya, the 'fox', that my father dedicated that portrait. Their relationship could have been the cause of the arguments and the crisis between my mother and father in 1973. Our families would have hushed the whole thing up and kept it from us for fear of a scandal. But that doesn't shed any light on the circumstances of your mother's death. In any case, it is unlikely that the relationship, if indeed there was one, was between Nataliya and Jean (who I'm going to visit tomorrow on the way back): he has always preferred boys.

Meet you in Paris? Yes, and with great pleasure. I didn't dare suggest it myself, not wanting to impose on you at a time like this. I'm planning to stop there overnight anyway, before driving on to Calais. I expect to arrive around 5 p.m. and can meet you in the evening. If you could suggest a good hotel not too far away from your place, and, if you are free, it would be my pleasure to invite you to dinner. I've actually decided to bring some of the albums back to England to sort them out at home. If we have time, we could look at some of them together.

I'll be on email until Friday morning.

With best wishes,

Stéphane

Dear Stéphane,

I can recommend Le Jardin Secret on Rue de Nancy, near the Gare de l'Est: clean, not too pricey and just around the corner from where I live. The easiest thing would be for you to come over when I get back from work, around 7.30 p.m. My culinary skills leave much to be desired, but I can feed you at least. Then we'll be able to look through the albums at our leisure. My door code is 284A. Don't hesitate to call if you have any problems.

In the meantime, safe journey, and hope the visit to your godfather goes well.

Can't wait to see you.

Hélène

6

She is lounging in a deck chair on a terrace surrounded by wrought-iron railings beyond which a silvery, sparkling triangle of sea can be glimpsed. Various objects are laid out at her feet: an open book with a damaged spine, a little canvas bag, a tube of sun cream and a lacquer cigarette lighter. A big umbrella in a plastic stand shields her from the afternoon sun; its tilt and the tautness of the fabric suggest a breeze is blowing. A few metres away, two children – a boy and a girl – are playing on the flagstones with what look like twigs. Behind the deck chair to the left is a white wrought-iron table, and on it is a large wooden tray with a domed metal cafetière, six china cups, a misted-up jug of water, a packet of Craven A – recognisable even though the camera angle has squashed the black cat logo – and a bowl of apricots. Sitting next to the table, a woman of around forty wearing trousers and a blouse is holding a spoon, a sign that tea is about to be served. There is another woman next to her, her corpulent frame squeezed into a summer frock that emphasises every roll of fat. She has put glasses on to count the rows of knitting in front of her, to which she devotes her full attention. She too is sheltering under an umbrella, a bigger one with stripes.

The young woman in the deck chair is wearing a typical 1960s dress with a wide rectangular neckline, bold geometric cut and diamond pattern. The straps of her bra which compresses her breasts are visible through the fabric. Her left arm is darker than the rest of the body, testifying to a recent touch of sunburn; her right hand rests on her belly. Only her swollen ankles protrude from beneath the light cotton throw covering her legs; her shoes dangle from her feet with the straps unbuckled, leaving a red mark on her skin. Her eyes are half shut, as if she is dozing; perspiration has slicked her thick hair to the side of her face, while the tortoiseshell comb has come loose, defeated.

The photograph has captured in its chemistry the blinding summer light falling vertically, flooding every pale surface it touches – the dress, the table, the little boy's cap. The image has the torpid, intense flavour of a summer afternoon, as confirmed by the words written on the back in Cyrillic, 'Динар, август 1968'. Moreover, seeing her in profile, it is difficult to ignore the fact that Nataliya Zabvina is at least eight months pregnant.

Paris, 7 September 2007

Dear Stéphane,

I hope you got back OK and that your trees were happy to see you again.

I'm so glad we were able to spend the evening together. I must admit I already had some idea of what to expect (physically, I mean) because I'd looked you up on your lab's website. But it goes without saying: the photo doesn't do you justice!

I already felt as if I knew you after reading your letters, but I hadn't realised just how alike we are and how many of the same demons we are fighting – which is a bit sad when you think about it. Sometimes I wonder what 'truth' it is we're chasing after exactly, and what kind of state it will leave us in if we find it.

Anyway, it was wonderful to chat over a good Bordeaux – the bottle you brought really was quite something – while we looked through the photos. It's not often I get the chance to talk to someone about all this and, in a selfish way, being able to share it with you has helped take the weight off me. I'm grateful for the time we spent together. If you're ever in Paris again, en route to Geneva or for work, do let me know.

After you left, I mulled over what you'd told me about the way Jean Pamiat reacted when he heard that we were in touch. It's hard to be sure what he meant, given his speech difficulties, but don't you think he might have been trying to tell you something about my mother?

Here, it's back to work (with a vengeance). I've been asked to edit the catalogues for two new exhibitions, one on the flooding of Paris in 1910, the other on working-class living conditions in the early 1900s, which I will also be curating. Very exciting projects, but I'm not quite sure how we're going to get it all done by Christmas.

We have already been sent eleven crates of archive material that I have begun to sift through. I always get the same spooky feeling when I catch the gaze of someone photographed a hundred years ago, looking back at you from beyond the grave. Often, the wording on the cards is charmingly quaint: 'a friend'; 'my parents join me in sending you their sincerest regards'; 'I thank you with all the respect I can muster' (honestly, I'm not making them up!)

All this means I might have quite a bit on my plate (to put it mildly) over the next few weeks, but I'll be sure to make time to nip over to Rue de la Mouzaïa and will let you know how I get on.

In the meantime, as little Geneviève says on the postcard, I'm sending you my 'sincerest regards'.

Hélène

Dear Hélène,

Thank you for your letter, which only arrived this morning, and for the colourful stamps which will brighten up my office. I am touched by what you say about our meeting, as I came away with the same feeling: that of sharing the burden at last. It's as if I've known you for years, and those few hours in Paris were all too brief for my liking.

My trees made no comment on my return, nor did they shake their little leaves, but I'd like to think they're pleased to see me. We're about to start a new programme, with a potential pharmaceutical application, and I too am likely to be swamped with work. I'm going away again at the end of the month for a series of seminars and a field trip to Finland.

For all these reasons, I haven't spent much time looking at the albums since I've been back. So far, all I've come across is a series taken on the Normandy coast. The photos are magnificent, but I don't have the foggiest idea what my father was doing there. So, like the inspector who follows Miss Marple to glean the fruits of her luminous discoveries, I'm waiting for the outcome of your visit to Rue de la Mouzaïa. And as I'm not as gifted as little Geneviève when it comes to pretty turns of phrase, I'll confine myself to an affectionate kiss if you don't mind.

Stéphane

PS The Bordeaux may have been magnificent, but the dinner wasn't bad either. Don't you dare tell me you're a hopeless cook!

Dear Stéphane,

I'm sorry it's taken me so long to get back to you. First I had to recover from the dreaded birthday party my friends sprang on me. And now, as predicted, I don't have a minute to myself with these two exhibitions to prepare. In the case of the one on the flood especially, we're drowning in documents (if you'll excuse the pun); we'll be up to our necks soon, like the Zouave statue on the Pont de l'Alma in Paris that's used as a high-water mark.

What with work and visits to Sylvia, who is now on permanent life support, I don't have much time to devote to our investigation. I haven't had a chance to carry on sorting things out at Rue de l'Observatoire. I have, however, been back to Rue de la Mouzaïa. The owners, a very nice young couple, showed me around, but they knew nothing about any of the previous occupants. Inside, it's just an ordinary modern house and I doubt that anything remains of the home Nataliya knew. I asked to see the courtyard: it's small, with no trees, and doesn't look like the one in the picture of the meal. But I did discover that the house is very close to Saint-Serge church, which I'll visit the next time I have a few hours to spare.

How about you? What have you been up to?

Hélène x

PS Nothing ventured, nothing gained: it was Sylvia, a true cordon bleu, who taught me to cook. Next time (if there is one), I'll make you a chocolate parfait.

Ashford, 29 September 2007

Dear Hélène,

You didn't tell me it was your birthday! I wish you a fortieth year filled with happiness. Happiness, and answers too.

By the way, if you promise me chocolate cake, not only might I come back, but what's more I'll book my train ticket right away!

Well, I'd love to, but the fact is I'm flying to Helsinki tomorrow, and I didn't want to leave without posting this letter.

You must write and tell me all about your visit to Saint-Serge, whose name conjures up for me all the splendours of imperial Russia.

Much love,

Stéphane

Dear Stéphane,

How are you? How's your teaching going in Helsinki? I'm longing to hear your news.

I have some of my own, as it happens. I went to Saint-Serge yesterday. It was an eventful day, to say the least!

First of all, I must tell you about the place; it's really quite amazing. It took me ages to find it, a little church tucked away in a grove of trees, at the top of a steep street. To get to it, you have to go up these strange wooden steps with latticed wooden panels either side. Every inch of the building is covered in paintings, embellished or decorated in some way. It makes you wonder how such an exotic, breathtaking structure ended up slap bang in the middle of Paris.

I was able to go inside the church, although in theory it was closed; by the looks of it there had just been a meeting, and a few people were still lingering. So I saw the iconostasis and the icons in the strangely low-ceilinged hall which was bathed in a mellow, womb-like light. I took some pictures of the outside for you, so you can see how spectacular it is.

One of the group, a lady in her fifties, noticed me standing there and came over to ask if I lived locally. I told her the reason for my visit and showed her the photo of the choir, which produced a curious Droste effect with the background of the picture reproduced life-size on the wall behind it. She examined the photo for a few seconds, turning it over. 'Yes,' she said, 'this picture was taken here, no doubt about it.' But she didn't recognise anyone in it – not surprising really, given her age. She must have read the disappointment on my face and suggested I go and see a woman by the name of Vera Vassilyeva, who had been very active in parish affairs and lived a bit further up, at the top of Rue de Crimée.

I went straight there, armed with the name of the woman I had spoken to and a note she had written on the back of a leaflet. When I rang the bell, the door opened as far as the safety chain would allow. Madame Vassilyeva, who looked like a wizened little imp, said nothing, but simply beckoned me to lean down towards her – she must be about four foot seven – and stared at me while I reeled off my explanation. Then she invited me in.

I would have put her down as being at least a hundred years old. Actually, she told me she's only ninety-two. She spoke a rather formal, broken French that she seemed to have learned during the imperial period, while I muddled along in my pidgin Russian. Nevertheless, we just about managed to understand one another. After going to great pains to make tea in a samovar at least as old as her, Vera motioned to me to sit down on a worn blue velvet sofa, staring fixedly at me again, her eyes hooded by her drooping lids.

Without thinking, I said in Russian, 'I am Nataliya Zabvina's daughter.'

It struck me how odd it was to be saying those words for the first time in my life, in that language, in that place, as though I was in the process of becoming another person.

Vera replied, 'I know.' Then, after a long silence broken only by her wheezing, 'You look like your mother.'

I felt my throat tighten. Sylvia aside, this was the first time since we started digging into all this that I'd spoken to someone who had known my mother. All at once Nataliya ceased to be a nebulous, shadowy figure and was once more flesh and blood, a voice, a presence. I showed Vera the photo and she tapped one of the faces with her gnarled finger: one of the three adults, the woman standing next to the priest. Her story was long and laboured, and she stopped several times to take a sip of tea, think, immerse herself in memories. But I was glad of these lulls in her account, as they gave me time to take in the shock of confronting the past.

From what I understood of Vera's story, and her memory seems to be intact, my mother's parents arrived in France soon after the end of the war. To begin with they lived in Sainte-Geneviève-des-Bois before they found a small, basic apartment on Rue de la Mouzaïa. According to Vera, my mother was very beautiful, loved music and sang in the parish choir. She had a friend who was older than her, 'Jan' (who must be Jean Pamiat), and they were always getting up to mischief together, smoking under the church steps or hiding a litter of newborn kittens behind the iconostasis. My grandfather's name was Oleg and my grandmother's Daria.

When they first arrived, Oleg took on all kinds of jobs – worker in a corset factory, gardener and then taxi driver. A year later, Daria took over, working as a cleaner while Oleg, at over forty, re-sat his medical exams, having lost some of his certificates in the exodus. And all the while he was battling to have the whole family granted French citizenship. Eventually they saved enough to rent a tiny flat with three rooms, one of which served as the consulting room. Business grew quickly and within a few years they were in a position to expand the practice. That's when the family left the 19th *arrondissement*. Vera couldn't remember exactly when they had moved, but she knew they had gone to live in the east of Paris.

Vera and my grandparents had continued to spend the summer holidays together until the distance came between them. Nataliya had returned to Saint-Serge several times to say hello to her old friends there. The last time she came, she was, Vera told me, *zamuzhem* – married – and carrying a babe in arms. 'Eto byla ty, eto byla ty' (it was you), the old woman said again and again, shaking her head and patting my arm. I looked into her eyes, faded and milky as they always are in the very elderly, the same eyes that thirty-nine years earlier had gazed on me in my mother's arms and had kept a mental photograph of that moment somewhere in the recesses of her mind, a photograph I would never see.

Vera knew that Nataliya had died: the priest at Saint-Serge had told her before the death notice went out. It was also the priest who told her a year or two afterwards that Dr Zabvine had passed away. 'Ot chego ona umerla?' (What did she die of?) – 'Ya ne znayu' (I don't know).

Just then, the old woman heaved herself out of her shabby armchair and, using a walking stick, made her way into another room. I could hear her opening doors and moving things around, muttering words in Russian I couldn't understand. I sat for more than a quarter of an hour in the autumnal gloom of the living room, the window casting an ever fainter rectangle of light. I asked myself what it is that forms the truth of a person, what happens when you grow up without memories, who were those people who had known me and of whom I knew nothing, whether some part of them – a word, an image, a smell – had stayed with me. *I am Nataliya Zabvina's daughter. Ya doch Natalii Zabviny.* The words in both languages kept going round and round inside my head, and repeating them to myself filled me with both fear and joy.

Eventually Vera Vassilyeva came back carrying a battered shoebox under her arm. She gestured to me to turn on the lamp, then she slumped into the armchair, out of breath, closing her eyes for a few seconds. Then she slowly lifted the lid and rummaged inside the box for several long minutes, her arthritic fingers leafing through old letters, notices and photos. Every now and then she would pick one out, saying 'Posmotri!' (look). There were images of the area in the 1940s, more photos of Saint-Serge, one featuring Jean Pamiat, a snapshot of a baby (me) held firmly by someone whose face wasn't visible, and a portrait of my grandparents. The seated woman at the lunch under the arbour was indeed my grandmother.

Then she paused and slowly took out a photo which she held towards me. 'Davay, posmotri!' I looked: it was my mother, pregnant.

With me, needless to say.

My past, which had always seemed so hazy and shapeless, suddenly had a face, pictured in such sharp focus that my heart skipped a beat. That's when I knew that the person who walked out the door of Vera Vassilyeva's apartment that day would no longer be quite the same Hélène Hivert who had walked in earlier.

It was dark when I left. I went for a brandy in the first bar I came across and the strength of the alcohol gradually brought me back to reality. I felt nauseous as I made my way home, sensing the onset of a migraine. When I got back to the flat, I felt as though I was returning from a voyage to the ends of the earth. Luckily Bourbaki was there: he has no interest whatsoever in my genealogical soul-searching, demanding only to be fed at set times.

Vera let me keep the picture of my mother. I look at this image which forces itself upon me, claiming my attention, and it makes my entire life seem fake, built on lies. The more I hear about Nataliya, the deeper the impression I form of her as a joyful, happy, well-loved person. What can have happened, what crime can she have committed to find herself so entirely wiped from family memory?

I'm going to write to the Paris medical council to find out where my grandfather Dr Zabvine practised, in the hopes of discovering others who might have known my mother. I'm sorry these new pieces in the puzzle don't tell us anything about your father, but I'm convinced they're part of a trail that will lead us to him.

If you have a few minutes, I'd love to hear your news.

Hélène
xxx

Dearest Hélène,

Forgive me for not writing sooner, the days are flying by (or rather the nights, I should say), and my trip has turned out to be rather demanding.

I was enthralled by the description of your visit to Saint-Serge. I think I understand how churned up you must be feeling and to some extent I share your emotion, at least partially. The more I've thought about these events, the fonder I've become of these two people about whom you and I knew so little. And like you I am on the hunt for the slightest scrap of information. Your encounter with this Madame Vassilyeva was a real stroke of luck: a place, a date, photos, new clues. And there is so much more for us to find out!

One thing intrigues me: where did you learn to speak Russian?

Here, everything is going very well. The students are delightful, keen, and my colleagues are very kind, although Finnish hospitality is somewhat reserved. The university has lent me an apartment not far from the campus, in the middle of the countryside, or almost, and I'm enjoying not having to be involved in the admin side of things. That said, I'll be glad to be home and eat real marmalade, and pick up my post.

Send my love to Bourbaki. And kisses to you.

Stéphane

Dear Stéphane of the Arctic,

Bourbaki says thank you and sends his love back. In fact, I had to lift him off the keyboard to write this.

Glad to hear all's going well. I envy you being up there in the remote northern reaches. Is there snow already?

In answer to your question, I learned a smattering of Russian at INALCO, the Oriental studies institute in Paris, where I took lessons for five years. I would describe my level as pretty elementary; I could never get my head around the verbs. But let's just say I know enough to tell the difference between a hamburger and caviar on a restaurant menu.

I have always felt drawn to the language, and I'm beginning to understand why. While I was learning Russian, certain words would strike me as strangely familiar, particularly strings of words like the names of the numbers, colours and days of the week. Weird associations too: the adjective *goluboy* always reminds me of a certain fabric, with beads and gold thread. The first time I heard the word *kotyonok*, a jumble of images came back to me: a bedcover, a fur throw. The same topsy-turvy sensation I once felt breathing in the perfume worn by the woman at the next table in a café in Aix-en-Provence, a scent I was sure I had inhaled as a small child. In other words, Proust's 'madeleine effect'.

One of my teachers once asked me if I had spoken Russian in the past or heard it spoken around me, and raised an eyebrow when I assured him I hadn't. It was one of those passing comments you put to the back of your mind without a second thought – until the day you realise what it meant.

If my mother was Russian, as her name suggests, she must of course have taught me these words when I was little, though I've since forgotten them.

She must have held me in her arms, sung to me, taught me to count, *odin, dva, tri, chetyre*, and I've forgotten all about it.

When are you coming home?

Love,

Hélène

Rovaniemi, 20 October 2007 (postcard)

Dear Hélène,

Fond wishes from Scandinavia. You who love the north, and the cold, you'd be like a duck in (frozen) water here.

All my love,

Stéphane

Paris, 23 October (email)

Dear Stéphane,

I don't know where this message will find you, but I wanted to let you know that Sylvia died last night. I'll write as soon as I can.

Hélène

Rovaniemi, 23 October (email)

Dearest Hélène,

I am so sorry. Words are useless in these situations, but I can imagine your grief, and I share your sorrow. Is there anything I can do for you at this distance? If nothing else, let me reassure you that you are constantly in my thoughts, even though we are far apart.

A big hug,

Stéphane

Dear Stéphane,

Thank you for phoning and please don't worry about calling so late. You did the right thing. It was so comforting to hear your voice. I had known for a while that Sylvia was going to die and in a way she had already left us, but it still came as a terrible shock. As I said, those final moments were ... difficult.

After all, she was my mother, even if she didn't give birth to me.

I'll be in touch soon.

Love,

Hélène

7

The sky is overcast but the sun is strong enough to shine through regardless. The dense cloud diffracts a series of slanting rays, visible to the naked eye, whose slow passage ends on contact with the water. Reflection upon reflection of late-afternoon light glazes the ebbing tide with a slick of liquid silver as it moves in ever lazier swirls, leaving flotsam, seaweed and shells stranded on the wet shore. The receding water does not prevent the sea from displaying its calm opulence, broken up by the crests of little waves streaking its surface with parallel lines. The beach is deserted. Only a couple and their dog disturb this elegy to emptiness. Or almost only: on looking closely, the tiny form of a child can be seen sitting on the beach playing with the sand (Where are its parents?). You can almost feel the bracing wind, the chill of the water, the density of the sand at last exposed to the air after a day in the relentless clutch of the waves.

In the top left-hand corner of the photo is the seafront with its imposing, harmonious facades, the fluid geometry of water pitted against the solid force of stone. A break in the ranks: a lone building rises up, with a gap on either side. The camera angle has foreshortened its impressive length, but nevertheless it dominates the landscape, its many chimneys giving it the appearance of a small chateau. Its two wings jut triumphantly towards the sea; they enclose a large glass conservatory, the beauty of the antique wrought ironwork defying the unperturbed majesty of the beach. It could be a casino, a railway station, a hotel: any one of those feats of early-twentieth-century seaside architecture, the setting for a novel bringing together a cast of cosmopolitan characters from Mitteleuropa. But for now, the sunlight bouncing off the water, the mercury-coloured beach, the tree-stump breakwaters, the solitude of idle stone are timeless, forming a moment suspended between land and sea where the muted light of an afternoon redolent of salt water and marine birds is gently fading.

Dear Stéphane,

I hope you'll forgive the long silence. Things have been pretty hectic following Sylvia's death and I still haven't finished dealing with all the formalities. At least it has kept me busy. I went back to work last week, which has also helped take my mind off things. As I said last time we spoke on the phone, no matter how much you're expecting it, it still comes as a shock. In the words of that song by Barbara, I feel like a (nearly) forty-year-old orphan.

Thankfully, at the very end, Sylvia was no longer aware of what was happening to her. She was cremated according to her wishes in a non-religious ceremony, and her ashes have been laid to rest beside my father's. Her brother came to the cremation, along with her surviving friends and a good turnout of former colleagues. It was a beautiful day; the sun shone on her final journey.

I've given up on our search for the time being; I don't feel up to it. I can only grieve for one person at a time. For now, all I want is to reflect on the woman who has just left us and who was no ghost, even if she did hide a great deal from me.

Please don't hold it against me.

I hope all's well with you and that you're happy to be back in England.

Love,

Hélène

Ashford, 21 November 2007

Dearest Hélène,

Thank you for taking the time to write. I was anxious to hear from you, although I realise that you must need time to yourself to adjust. I well remember that feeling from when my father died last year. That initial shock of being alone from now on, the panic of the survivor who knows that it will be their turn next in the natural order of things. And for you, having no siblings, it is probably even harder.

With time, that feeling has faded, it's become less ... violent. It will be the same for you, I think. It is the transition that seems to drag on.

And of course I don't hold it against you. Why would I? Sylvia was there for you during most of your childhood and then your adult years. I think that putting your grief for her before mourning the death of a young woman in a fifty-year-old photo is a very healthy reaction. The living first, shadows second. You told me that when you left Vera's house you were haunted by the feeling that your life had been a lie, a fabrication. Whatever you were told or not told, every one of your letters seems to confirm one thing beyond all doubt: your parents loved you. And on that point, lying is not possible. You can't deceive a child over the quality of your love for them for thirty-nine years.

I know that this probably isn't the time for an invitation, but if you feel that a few days away from Paris would help you to get through this difficult period, my house is open to you.

Affectionately,

Stéphane

PS In the 'Brittany 1968' album I found a series of seaside photos. I don't know why the beauty of one of them affected me so deeply, but I immediately felt I wanted to send it to you, because it is so peaceful. The water, the light, the sand, that building: time cannot alter a landscape of such perfection. My father really was an extraordinary photographer. What a pity he didn't seek recognition for his work.

Paris, 27 November 2007

Dear Stéphane,

I really appreciate your thoughtful offer, but it's still a bit soon for me; I don't think I'd be very good company. For the time being, work is helping me cope (which is lucky, since I've got mountains of it). But if you can hold the invitation open a little while, I can think of nothing I'd like better than to pay you a visit. I'm curious to see where you live, along with your garden filled with weird trees.

You're right, my parents did love me. I sometimes had doubts about my father, who could be quite tetchy and distant, but they passed. He was an army man who wasn't very demonstrative either verbally or physically. Even at the end of his life when he was very ill, I found it difficult to touch him. Sylvia told me that when I was little, I sometimes addressed him as 'vous' instead of 'tu', I was so in awe of him. Occasionally he would fly into a violent rage (like the time he snatched my Red Army Choir record, which I used to play on a loop in my bedroom as a teenager, and snapped it in two), and I'm beginning to understand why. With hindsight, I think he was a man who had suffered a lot but didn't want to show it.

Thank you for the photo. Two of the albums you left with me are full of pictures taken in Brittany, and I browse through them often: your father managed to capture the light, the rugged character, the mineral beauty of the place. He must have had a real fondness for the region. I can tell you what's in the picture: it's the Grand Hôtel des Thermes in Saint-Malo – an iconic building, right on the waterfront. Every now and then I head up there for a couple of days' break from the noise and chaos of Paris. There is indeed something eternal about the place.

Love,

Hélène

Dear Stéphane,

I had a nightmare last night. You and Sylvia were deep in conversation, and she was telling you that my father had been away too often.

I haven't slept properly for weeks; I keep turning things over in my mind. Especially something Sylvia said before she died, very clearly, in Russian, which meant something like, 'the child has forgotten her birth'. She used a distinctive form, *zapamyatovala*, which is a variant of the verb 'to forget' and literally means 'she has put it behind her memory'. I don't know what she was trying to tell me, or which child she had in mind. Those were her last intelligible words.

I heard from her solicitor yesterday. He wants to meet me to read the will. Words like that bring her death home to me almost more brutally than the death itself. I miss Sylvia. But then I'd been missing her for years.

Winter has taken hold of Paris: it's snowing, and the overground section of the métro was completely white this morning. I like this cotton-wool coating, this watery velvet: it slows the city down, makes it more human. Normally I run out and take pictures, but this time I'm just standing looking at it.

I'm sorry this letter is rather gloomy. I wish I had more cheerful news. It will come soon, I hope. I think of you often.

Hélène

Dear Hélène,

I often think of you too, and feel a little concerned right now. Are you sure you don't want to come and visit me in Ashford? Bourbaki is invited too, if his vaccinations are up to date; he can act as chaperone.

There's another option, which may sound a little casual when you are in mourning, but here goes: would you like to join me for Christmas and New Year in Geneva? I normally go for ten days and spend Christmas with Philippe and his partner Marie. They'd be delighted to have us to stay, and you can be sure they'll welcome you without making assumptions.

It would also be an opportunity to show you the entire collection of photographs, which I wasn't able to do in August, and for you to have a change of scene, if you like winter walks. I know how emotionally difficult the first Christmas without one's parents can be, and perhaps a short break in a new place would be a way of cushioning your grief.

But you probably have hundreds of friends who have already invited you to spend the holidays with them.

I came across something rather strange in the album, but I feel uncomfortable bothering you with that at present. Let me know when you feel like talking about it again.

A big hug,

Stéphane

Dear Stéphane,

I would have taken up your invitation without making assumptions, as you put it :-) The prospect of a winter break in Switzerland and going for walks in the snow would have helped lift my spirits. But I'm afraid I've already agreed to go to Germany for the holidays, and I can't really get out of it. Thank you for thinking of me, though — I'm really touched. Will you be coming via Paris, like last time?

In the meantime, please do tell me what it was that piqued your curiosity. Now it's me who's curious.

Love,

Hélène

PS I received a reply today from the general medical council, in answer to the letter I sent them before Sylvia died. They confirm there was indeed an ophthalmologist by the name of Dr Oleg Zabvine on their books. He practised first at 142 Rue de la Mouzaïa between 1954 and 1959, and then at 22 Rue Marsoulan in the 12th *arrondissement* from 1959 to 1973. Vera Vassilyeva was spot on.

Ashford, 6 December 2007

Dear Hélène,

What a pity you won't be able to join us! I would have loved to take you on some mini hikes to show you 'our' winter. Unfortunately, I'm flying to Geneva this time, as the Shuttle was fully booked. Much to my chagrin, I won't be stopping off in Paris.

The thing that intrigued me – to put it mildly – was to discover the 'twin' of the photo that Vera Vassilyeva gave you. I found it in the album that my father made in Brittany in 1968. It is almost the identical image, taken within a few minutes, or even a few seconds of the other one. I can't understand how it ended up there. But there is something alarming about the coincidence that made these two photos surface at almost the same time, when they had been lying forgotten for forty years in two different places, so far from each other.

All my love, and I hope to see you very soon.

Stéphane

Dear Stéphane,

How odd. I can't think of an explanation for it either, and shan't try to find one for the time being. If something occurs to me, I'll let you know.

At least twenty centimetres of snow has fallen here, making Paris unusually silent; all you can hear is the muffled sound of cars crawling past and the scraping of street cleaners' shovels clearing the pavements. The overground part of the métro is totally white. I went for a walk in the Buttes-Chaumont yesterday morning, wearing my wellies and wrapped up like an Eskimo, and I took some pictures for you. I love winter; over the years it has become my favourite season. This winter, which has blanketed my sadness, has me completely spellbound.

I need to snap out of it though, because the disruption of the last few weeks has thrown the catalogue way off schedule.

I keep putting off going to see Sylvia's solicitor. I still haven't phoned him back.

To be honest, I'm not really looking forward to

visiting my friends in Germany either. I would have liked to come to Geneva, and I'm more eager than ever to look at the rest of the photo collection. From the little I've seen of your father's work, it seems to me that you and your brother might consider exhibiting it – it really is that good. I could help you find a venue in Paris, if you like.

You'll be gearing up to leave by the time this letter arrives. So I'll take this opportunity to wish you a wonderful trip to Geneva, a merry Christmas and a very happy New Year.

Love,

Hélène

1 January, 00:04 (text message)

Wishing you a very happy New Year! And all good things, as we say here. 2008 kisses. Stéphane.

1 January, 01:17 (text message)

A very happy New Year to you too from Göttingen!
Love, Hélène xxxxxxxxxxxxxxxxxxxxxxxxxxxxx (and
so on to infinity!)

8

The background is a pale, sober grey: no clouds, no manicured garden, stucco columns or painted benches. Just four people captured in the same small space at the same moment. Two adults and two children. They are bathed in a gentle light which smooths their skin, softens their features and makes their hair look thick and lustrous. A woman is standing on the left of the picture: average height, light-coloured eyes and fair hair in two thick braids wound around her head. Her blond eyelashes are invisible, giving her a fixed, vulnerable stare that belies the broad open smile lighting up her thin face. The rest of her body, encased in a well-cut white shift dress, is muscular, compact, well-defined: she looks the sporty type, a keen walker scaling mountainsides with sure, solid strides. She holds the taller boy by the shoulder. He, like his brother (presumably), is wearing a short trouser suit. The elder boy's hair has been Brylcreemed and parted on the left and a comb has left clear, evenly spaced grooves furrowed through the blond mass. He is smiling shyly but there is a far-off look on his face as he stands constricted by the too-tight jacket and tie.

The smaller boy has been sat on a chair to avoid unbalancing the picture with too great a height difference. He is openly laughing and the position of his leg, with the toe of his ankle-boot sticking out, suggests he must have fidgeted as the shutter closed. One of his hands is clamped in his brother's; the other is outstretched, open-palmed, like a toddler's. The velvet bow tie around his neck has slipped; one of his cotton socks is corkscrewing downwards and a cascade of unruly ringlets frames the moon-shaped face of a cheeky little prince. He is not looking at the camera, as he must have been instructed, but to one side, gazing up at the man on his left.

The man has put on a dark suit and plain tie for the occasion. He, too, has Brylcreemed his hair, though it has done nothing to repress the thick, curly mane — now several centimetres longer. The fingertips of his white, bony hand brush the shoulder of the little boy without exercising the slightest restraint. The classic attire and upright, serious stance cannot mask a certain irony in the body, which knows itself to be attractive and exudes an unexpected arrogance. Yet the suggestion of a smile, or — who can tell? — a trace of bitterness in his eyes shows he has not wholeheartedly embraced the photographic ritual he has himself orchestrated, but is doing his best to honour it.

He is standing back, ever so slightly removed from the other three — a matter of centimetres, no more. In haste, no doubt, to take up his place after pressing the timer button, returning to a pre-arranged position. And to make chemistry responsible for assigning roles on glossy paper, becoming, once and for all, the father of his children.

Dear Hélène,

How are you? Did you have a good holiday in Germany? What did Bourbaki get for Christmas?

I arrived back from Geneva on Saturday after a very enjoyable family holiday. My brother Philippe is a charming person, with a terrific sense of humour too, and I'm very fond of him; he's the one who's got the photography gene, but as an amateur (he's an architect by profession). I'd love you to meet him; I'm sure you'd get on like a house on fire.

Since I flew, I wasn't able to bring back as many albums as last time, but it's a good crop. Not so much for our investigation, but rather for me: I found a series of family photos, taken around 1969–70. All four of us are in the shots, which was very unusual. I'll send you one, as a curio, or a sociological sample, whatever you prefer to call it, of what a model Swiss family looked like (outwardly, at least). Of course you'll recognise yours truly in the well-scrubbed little boy to the left of the picture – please don't laugh.

I found another series taken in Brittany, but dated

1970 this time, with incredible views of the grand hotel you told me about and which I now dream of visiting. The place is straight out of a Vicki Baum novel (yes, I admit it, I read 'hotel novels'. Promise me you won't tell anyone.)

Put on an exhibition? Why not? Like you I believe that the photos are easily as good as those of some fine art photographers: the Brittany albums alone make an excellent series. My father was a fervent admirer of Atget, and he took inspiration from him in choosing certain angles for his shots. Extraordinary shapes, a particular way of capturing emptiness, the silence of surfaces. Our investigation has given me the opportunity to rediscover his work and to think differently about this man who seemed to be fascinated by the absence of any human life.

Love,

Stéphane

Dear Stéphane,

Before I go any further, there are two things I simply must tell you: 1) You're irresistible in short trousers and 2) If ever you feel like starting up a Vicki Baum fan club, count me in. I've read every single one of her books.

My holiday went well, thank you, and I'm glad to hear yours did too. I cut my trip to Germany short by a few days; I didn't much feel like being around people, so I came back to Paris to give Boubou his Christmas present – lots of cuddles (the big fatty doesn't deserve anything else after living off a diet of non-stop treats at my neighbour's).

I made the most of my unexpected free time to visit Rue de l'Observatoire. I don't know if you've read anything by the German novelist, W. G. Sebald; he wrote a short story about the body of a guide frozen inside a glacier and spat out again decades later. My father's study is starting to have the same effect on me.

I went over some of the lower shelves with a fine-tooth comb, followed by the ones at the very top. That's where I got another surprise in the shape of a black archive box fastened with cord, of the kind used in libraries – and in fact, it still had its class mark and label on. The only thing inside was a parcel sent from Geneva in January 1973 with no return address. An unsealed letter was enclosed with the kind of flat metal tin you'd put biscuits or sweets in. This is what it said:

> Having been at the hospital at the time of her death, I was able to collect your wife's personal effects, which I am now returning to you. Nataliya was my dearest friend and an extraordinary person, and we have all been left devastated by her death. May I take this opportunity to extend my deepest sympathies to you and your little daughter Hélène at this terribly sad time. Jean Pamiat.

The address on the label informs me my parents were living in Brest at the time, at 71 Rue Félix-Gray.

The string around the tin had not even been undone, and I started to tremble as I went to cut it. I gathered everything up and brought it home with me and have so far left it untouched. So it's true, Nataliya died in an accident in Geneva. And my father wasn't there. Could she have been with yours? Do you think there's any way at all of communicating with Jean Pamiat to try to find out more?

Love,

Hélène

Dear Hélène,

Jean is too frail to be able to explain anything, but I'm going to talk to him about the parcel when I next visit him, asking questions to which he can simply reply yes or no. I promise you.

If Nataliya died in Geneva in January 1973, that would explain my father's grim mood from that year on. But in 1973, as far as I can remember, he was still living at home. Unless his absences for photographic expeditions served to cover up a parallel existence.

You might find other clues when you investigate the contents of the box. Above all, be sure to keep me posted.

Love,

Stéphane

Dear Stéphane,

Even though I desperately wanted to know what was inside, I really had to force myself to open the tin. The dry string snapped clean in half the moment I touched it. I had the same uneasy feeling I had experienced at Vera Vassilyeva's, the same impression of shadows becoming flesh. And the same sense that everything I had taken for granted was revealing itself to be utterly counterfeit. I took in the contents of the box half-fascinated, half-nauseous.

I am now in possession of Nataliya's wedding ring – which they must have removed before she was cremated – engraved with the words 'Michel and Nathalie, 1 February 1968'. Another ring, made from guilloched silver, carries an inscription in Russian: 'Σд уём пфидёшь, то и наидэшь', meaning something along the lines of 'seek and ye shall find'. Oh, the irony! If you look closely at your father's self-portrait, you'll see he's wearing the same ring, or one exactly like it, around his neck. A rectangular blue-lacquered cigarette lighter monogrammed 'NZ'; a faded tortoiseshell comb;

round glasses with a broken lens and a strange serpent bracelet which I might have played with as a child – it vaguely rings a bell.

The tin also contained a wallet, whose leather had hardened and cracked at the edges. It must have lain untouched for thirty-five years and I felt I was committing an act of sacrilege by rifling through it. Inside I found an identity card, still registered to Rue de la Mouzaïa, a passport, a reader's card for Sainte-Geneviève library issued in 1971, and some first-class métro tickets. One of them had a phone number written on the back, without a name. And then there was a picture of me as a baby, the same one I had seen at Vera Vassilyeva's.

The last thing left in the bottom of the tin was a 1972 diary. Its cover was completely falling apart, as if the leather had been slashed with something sharp. There's very little written in it: the address of a military base in Nouméa, some initials ('P.', 'I.': Pierre? Interlaken?) and arrows across the dates when my father was away. While most of the notes are in French, in April 1972 Nataliya wrote a word in Cyrillic, quite a complicated one. According to my dictionary, it means something like 'hydrotherapy clinic'. To treat what illness? Whatever it was, it's clear to me she was keen to hide mention of this trip from my father, hence her writing it in Russian. October and November contain several telephone numbers, one of which (the same one on the métro ticket) is in the centre of a page, underlined. And a meeting with a certain Maître Niemetz on 26 October. A divorce lawyer?

She has marked certain dates with crosses every four or five weeks, but after September they disappear. In the addresses section at the back, there is a list of names, most of which I've never heard of, with the exception of Vera Vassilyeva, Jean and Sylvia M. (my Sylvia, I think). An address with no name (284 Rue Suzanne-Lilar), an appointment with no details besides the time (3 p.m.) on 17 November, and then nothing. She must have been torn from this life so brutally.

For the moment, I'm not sure what to make of these new finds. But they have taught me one thing: the intensity of my father's hatred or indifference towards my mother, since he didn't even bother to open the tin. Such total rejection is hard to comprehend. That was a real shock.

I spent a long while turning Nataliya's things over in my hands with a kind of superstitious fervour. Of course, I couldn't resist trying on her jewellery and even putting her glasses on. She was very short-sighted: through the lens that's still intact, the world looks tiny and distorted. An asthma attack put an end to my game and I had to wait for my inhaler to kick in before I could write to you.

Does anything in this sorry contents list mean anything to you?

Hélène x

Ashford, 14 January (email)

Dear Hélène,

Yes, I recognise two things: my father always used to wear that ring on a chain around his neck, and Philippe must still have it somewhere. I'd never noticed that it was engraved. As for Rue Suzanne-Lilar, it's in Lausanne; I know because I have sometimes parked there. The online directory tells me there's now a rehab centre at that address; I'm going to email them to find out how long they've been there. Maybe you could try and track down this lawyer Niemetz.

Next time we see each other, for I hope we'll see each other soon, would you show me that diary? It is possible that I might recognise some names, even telephone numbers, you never know.

But above all, think of your own needs and look after your health. This investigation is affecting you deeply, perhaps too deeply, and your body is giving you a warning. Take care, dear Hélène.

Love,

Stéphane

Dear Stéphane,

I don't know how to tell you this. I know I must write this message and find the courage to send it, but I am already dreading the consequences.

I had another nightmare last night — a jumble of photos, my mother's wedding ring, snippets of conversations we've had and in particular something you said about an image being the twin of another — and I think I have worked out what Sylvia was trying to say before she died.

The child is me, and the 'forgotten birth' is where I come from.

Not geographically. Genetically.

If you think about it, it all adds up. Our parents had known each other at least ten years. We're almost certain they had an affair. Both happened to be in the same place in the same year: your father took hundreds of pictures of Brittany in 1968, and he passed through Saint-Malo. The photo of my mother pregnant was taken in Dinard, which is a few minutes away by boat or car. And it must have been taken by Pierre. That's why there are two copies: the one Vera showed me and the one in the 'Brittany 1968' album.

I dug out my father's sketchbooks and started doing some calculations. I was born on 10 September 1968, which means I must have been conceived in early December 1967. Yet my parents were only married on 1 February; we know that from the wedding ring. Not only that, but the series of drawings my father made in Nouméa, New Caledonia, begin on 13 November of the previous year and carry on until *mid-January* (I suppose he must have come back to get married) at the rate of two or three entries a week. Therefore he was not in Europe at the beginning of that winter, yet in the picture taken the following August, my mother is clearly right at the end of her pregnancy.

There are two possible explanations: either I was born prematurely, or Michel Hivert is not my father. And if not him, who else could it be but Pierre Crüsten? Everything seems to point to him. Might Nataliya have confessed the truth at some point, or did a physical resemblance give the game away as I was growing up? That would explain everything: the shame surrounding her memory and the severity of your parents' marital problems, assuming your mother had found out (an affair can be forgiven, but a child is another matter). Not to mention my father's aloofness towards me which, if he knew I wasn't his daughter, suddenly makes sense.

I'm trying to reason with myself, to convince myself this is nothing but a mesh of ludicrous theories. I'm afraid of being proved right. The implications would be just ... unthinkable.

Help me to see clearly.

Hélène
x

Ashford, 17 January (email)

Dearest Hélène,

You're mistaken. What you say is not true. It isn't possible. My father had many faults, but he would never have abandoned a child (you in this case). And even less after your mother's sudden death. Your theory doesn't hold water for a second.

You are not my half-sister and I am not your half-brother. You must get that absurd notion out of your head. I understand that you're very upset by what you have discovered and by Sylvia's death, but don't allow yourself to get carried away by ridiculous suppositions. They only tarnish the memory of our parents and are not at all helpful. And if that's the kind of conclusion we're going to come to, perhaps we'd better stop now.

Stéphane

Paris, 17 January (email)

Message received and understood. If it makes you feel any better, I wasn't exactly keen to be your sister either — I'm past the age of fantasising about long-lost siblings.

Hélène

Dear Hélène,

January is drawing to a close and I'm ending the month with a heavy heart. I've been turning the words over and over in my mind for days on end without being able to find a way to express what I want to say.

I apologise for what I wrote to you two weeks ago.

My reply was terse and hurtful, and you didn't deserve that. What's more it was a stupid thing to say, since we are both certain that our parents had an affair, so why not a child together? We are gradually piecing together their story, and we can't pick and choose only the bits we like.

To tell you the truth, the idea that we could be related caused me great disappointment. Disappointment at the idea that my father could have been a selfish, thoughtless man and a liar, who refused to take responsibility for the child he had fathered. An affair, I could imagine, but that, no, not at all.

Disappointment too, as I thought about all that pointless suffering: mine and Philippe's (ultimately, were we not merely obstacles to my father's happiness, a family as a sort of stop-gap or a source of regret?), your father's, if he realised the situation, and your own.

And, above all, consternation at the thought that the bond that has been growing between us these past months should so abruptly have to switch to a different kind of affection.

Now, I, too, have had time to think. And I still believe that you are wrong about the chain of events. Agreed, all the clues stack up. But that does not rule out the possibility of another explanation! Sylvia said something to you about birth and a child, I know, but she was dying, and suffering from Alzheimer's too: how lucid is a person in that situation? You worked out the dates, fair enough. Except that many, many babies are born prematurely, and it is impossible to calculate the exact stage of a pregnancy from a simple photograph. Supposing Pierre and Nataliya saw each other again in December in Brittany, which we don't know for sure – your mother lived in Paris! – they might not necessarily have resumed their affair straight away ... and besides, given the times, especially in a religious family like yours, a wedding was nearly always preceded by a formal engagement period. Would Nataliya have had a lover during that time? You have to admit that there is a serious inconsistency there, which also applies to any suspicions you may have about an extramarital affair.

There is still the photo, the most delicate point, but also the one that most clearly supports my theory. Let's imagine for a moment that my father, on a trip to Brittany, found out, from Jean Pamiat, for example, that Nataliya was on holiday in the area. He might have felt it was permissible to go and say hello to an old friend, now married and expecting her first child. Nothing reprehensible about that! Do you think he'd have taken the risk of showing up in front of your grandmother Daria and family friends if they'd been lovers? In my opinion, he must simply have taken a few photos as a memento of that afternoon. He would then, out of courtesy, have sent a set to Vera, one to Nataliya, and have kept one for his personal collection. Unless Pierre was never there and it was quite simply Jean who was the photographer.

The photos we have suggest that something must have happened between them *after* your birth; of that I am convinced. But that they should have had a child at that point in their respective lives doesn't add up as far as I can see. And besides, you don't look at all like my father or Philippe, or like me either.

There is one way to set our minds at rest, and that is to have a mitochondrial DNA test, which works for people who have one or two parents in common. I'm not an expert in animal biology, but I have some good colleagues and I know how to read a result. I enclose a testing kit. If you courier it back to me, we'll have the answer within a few days. Please forgive my churlish reaction to your theory. I can appreciate your reasoning even if I am resisting it energetically. But perhaps that's a lot to ask.

Your friend in spite of everything,

Stéphane

Dear Stéphane,

Yes, I was hurt by what you said, although I must take a share of the blame for blurting out my theory in an email, which I should never have done.

I'm just as dismayed by the idea as you are and, I now feel able to say, for the same reasons. We've known each other almost a year now and I think of you often — and not just in the way one thinks about a brother. (As I write these words I see that I will have to live with their consequences. Too bad. I owe it to you to be open by now.)

Even so, I still don't think my theory is as absurd as all that. The situation for women in 1968 was a lot more complicated than it is today. The bill to legalise contraception had only just been passed and had not yet come into effect; abortion was illegal and usually carried out in appalling conditions. Supposing Nataliya fell pregnant by Pierre during her engagement (and who's to say she didn't bring the wedding forward to avoid a scandal?), she would hardly be the first woman to try to pass off another man's child as her husband's.

And it's quite possible your father would have known nothing about it, which would explain why he showed no interest in me.

The test is the only way to know for sure. I have followed all the instructions to the letter, so I hope the sample will be good enough to use.

Let me know as soon as you get the results.

Hélène

Paris, 10 February (email)

Dear Stéphane,

Thank you, thank you a thousand times for your phone call. You have no idea how relieved I am. And happy, what's more. We said some things we'll need to come back to, but for now the only thought in my mind is relief for both of us in knowing this: we are not brother and sister.

Hélène
x

Dearest Hélène,

I'm relieved too. And happy. Very.

The rest, yes, we need to talk about it. And this time, we could avoid emailing, which I don't think is the best way of having this conversation. When and where?

Kisses,

Stéphane

Dear Stéphane,

I've gone ahead and made a reservation for this coming Saturday at the Grand Hôtel des Thermes de Saint-Malo, where two rooms await us for the weekend. As you know, it's a glorious place. I'm sure we will be made to feel very much at home there.

Hélène

17 February (text message)

Dearest Hélène, I'm back home filled with the memory of you. I hope you have no regrets. Perhaps this will come to nothing, perhaps it was just a parenthesis, perhaps we can't hope for anything more. But it was so … extraordinary. Thinking of you, Stéphane

Paris, 17 February (email)

Dear, dear Stéphane,

No regrets, as the song goes …

I knew when you came to see me in Paris it would happen sooner or later. I think we both did, didn't we?

The thought was there, lodged in the back of my mind. It never left me. Even the day Sylvia died. In fact I think it was what gave me the strength to keep going.

As I have come to know you better, I've felt increasingly as if you have always been part of my life. You have been a place of refuge, a place I could breathe, someone who, like me, had been through loneliness and come out the other side. Though I sensed your eagerness, I was in no hurry to come to you; in a way, we were already together.

I don't know what the future holds for us either, Stéphane. But yesterday morning when I saw you arrive outside the Grand Hôtel des Thermes, I realised I couldn't imagine being without you, and your eyes told me you felt the same way too. Let's pray we never have to be apart.

Hélène

II
LIGHT

Men, brother men, that after us live,
Let not your hearts too hard against us be
François Villon

9

The sky is clear, but the wan light indicates that the season is moving towards autumn. There is an almost tangible chill hanging over the mound with its patchy grass, stone bench, time-worn crucifix and former chapel whose steps are now overgrown with weeds and brambles, from which a rusty arch emerges. A prolific wisteria that is beginning to fade completely conceals one of the walls, and its invasive, interwoven branches compete with an ivy for the territory. Both contrive to hide the base of the cross adorning the roof. At the left end of the stone seat in front of the disused chapel sits a woman, her legs crossed. Her face is slightly rounded, especially her cheeks; her body has lost its angular sharpness. A round, black felt hat, slightly too big for her, partly covers her hair, now mid-length but still as abundant, drawn back in a ponytail. She is wearing a white blouse and a thick, shapeless woollen waistcoat. A pair of glasses with round metal frames dangle from a string around her neck, and an oversize reefer jacket, probably belonging to a man, is draped across her shoulders, its sleeves falling across her chest. She is slightly hunched, withdrawn, her legs crossed, lost in a voluminous woollen skirt from which a thread hangs, caused by a tiny snag. The mud stains on her ordinary flat-heeled loafers suggest she has hiked up to this spot.

The model is not looking at the photographer. Even though she is facing the camera, her eyes are elsewhere, lost in thoughts whose content we cannot fathom. Between the fingers of her wedding-ring hand, palm pressing on the stone edge, is an unlit cigarette. Her other hand absently fiddles with the little chain around her neck, the tip of her index finger hooked over it and partly hiding the ring suspended from it. Is it the frontal nature of the shot, the harsh light, that breaks up the surfaces and hardens her features? The thin grass and the wind bothering her? The photograph, which was probably to be a memento of a shared moment, does the precise opposite: it is pure solitude. Nathalie Hivert's face is transfixed, drained by a subdued melancholy that leaves on its surface only a coating of plaster-like heaviness. And her faraway gaze, lost in invisible wanderings, is the poignant symptom of a distress that nothing could mask or quell. This time, all the efforts of silver nitrate, gelatin, developers and paper are useless. Despite the photonic imprint stolen from her on that autumn day, that woman was already gone.

Ashford, 18 February (email)

Dearest Hélène,

What are you doing, what are you reading, what's going on in your life?

And if you don't have other plans, would you come to Geneva with me next weekend? As I said to you on the phone, Jean is asking for me all the time.

All my love,

Stéphane

Paris, 18 February (email)

Dear Stéphane,

As if you had to ask! Yes I will Yes, as Molly Bloom would say, come with you to Geneva. And we can stop off to see Jean on the way back; I'm dying to meet him. Did the nurse tell you exactly what happened?

I'll be waiting for you at the flat on Friday. You know the way, but you'll need the new magic number: B220.

A tender kiss,

Hélène

Dearest Hélène,

It was so hard to say goodbye last night. I envy Bourbaki, who must have taken advantage to hog the other pillow (that cat thinks he owns the place). The weekend went like a dream: Philippe and Marie thought you were delightful. And they're right, because you are. On the other hand, I don't think they believed in our ... 'friendship' – strange the discretion that makes us keep our relationship secret, as if we ourselves were afraid to believe in it.

Here, my trees can make eyes at me, but all I can think about are yours (eyes, not trees), and you have no idea how much the thought of this three-week field trip to Hawaii is getting me down. I leave in four days, when really I want to do the exact opposite, i.e. whizz over to Paris and join you, instead of flying off to the other side of the world. I do hope you'll be good enough not to forget me while we're apart.

When I got back, I opened the envelope that Jean's nurse had given me; I should have taken the opportunity to do so on our last evening, but I had other things on my mind, as you'll have noticed, and I more or less decided to leave the envelope unopened. I'm sorry you weren't allowed to see my godfather when we visited him, but he was too agitated to concentrate on a conversation. He was very anxious to get me to understand what he wanted to give me.

His nurse eventually found the object among his things: a large, thick, brown notebook in which he kept a diary (I didn't know he had this habit). The volume I have is from 1972–3. But I can't read it, because he wrote the whole thing in Russian. Although I don't know the Cyrillic alphabet very well, I think I can recognise the name 'Natasha', which recurs often. I also found, in glassine paper, a series of negatives, but I'm not sure what they represent: a snowscape? I have taken them to an elderly photographer in London to develop. He's charging a small fortune given the age of the film, but he's promised to print them within three days.

So I'll Fedex the diary and the prints to you before I leave. Do you think you'll be able to translate it? Or have it translated? I am almost certain that it contains the key to our mystery.

But, for the time being, the mystery I'd like to resolve is the one that would enable me to turn the clocks forward. I miss you, Hélène.

Stéphane xxxxxxx

PS I've finally heard back from the rehab centre in Rue Suzanne-Lilar, who I wrote to last month. They did some research: in 1972, it was a general medical practice.

Ashford, 28 February 2008

In haste, before I leave, here's Jean's notebook. Wasn't able to collect the photos in time to send them to you. I'll pick them up on the way to the airport.

I'll be thinking of you.

A thousand kisses,

Stéphane

Dear Stéphane,

Thank you for that long phone call from the other side of the world, which must have bankrupted you. I'm picturing you now sipping a long drink on the beach, turquoise waters lapping at your feet, enjoying the company of some voluptuous local woman. A cliché, I know! You lucky thing, invited to spend three weeks on an island paradise and all you can think about is getting back to Europe.

OK, I'm winding you up but 1) I'm flattered and 2) I can't wait for you to come home either. I'm like a child counting down the days on the calendar. Honestly, at our age!

Your Fedex parcel arrived safe and sound. Only a thousand kisses? That's not many, but I suppose I'll have to make do. Joking aside, I've begun to flick through the diary. It does indeed talk about my mother. But I'm not used to the cursive writing and I'm finding it very tricky to decipher. It took me almost an entire evening to transcribe the first two pages. The Russian is quite complex and I'm only understanding about one word in three. You said your godfather spoke Russian, but are you sure he wasn't in fact Russian, or born into a Russian-speaking family?

So far I've managed to work out that the beginning of the diary talks about photographic jobs and somebody called Friedrich, who's supposed to come to Geneva but doesn't turn up.

The edges of the last page had been glued to the back cover to make a pocket. I carefully slit one side open with a Stanley knife. Inside, I found a photo of my mother, which I've scanned and attached. There's no place or date written on the back.

Nataliya must be thirty-something in the picture, which would tally with the dates of the diary entries. But how sad she looks. She could be a different person from the bubbly girl in the choir photo and at the lunch. She doesn't look well. Since she mentions a clinic twice in her diary, I wonder whether she was ill. If the whole accident story was not yet another lie to cover up the real reason for her death. A 'shameful' disease, as people used to say? Or tuberculosis, which was kept strictly hidden from children?

I've sent an email to Boris, one of my lecturers at the language school, and I'll go and see him this week. He's bilingual and has agreed to translate the diary for me for a fee. We'll have to wait a little while for it, but it'll be much quicker than trying to do it myself.

With a bit of luck, we'll have it in time for your return.

If I were playing the game and being tactical, I should probably feign a certain indifference, but I'd be wasting my time: I miss you terribly.

Kisses, my globetrotter,

Hélène

PS How about you? Have you had time to look at the photos?

Hawaii, 2 March (email)

Aloha, my love!

While it's probably grey in Paris, I'm basking in the sun on my forty-fourth-floor balcony, sipping a chemical concoction so full of sugar that my blood-glucose level is alarming.

There's an unobstructed view over the island's biggest car park, I think, with a patch of blue that looks vaguely like the sea at the far end. I'm struggling with the jet lag. Classes start the day after tomorrow. This afternoon my American colleague and I are meeting for a guided tour of part of the city, if I've understood correctly.

No time to look at the photos, which remained in my checked-in suitcase during the journey. I'll write more about them as soon as I can. As for the photo you sent me, that chapel looks familiar; I'm sure I've been there before. But when?

On that note, I'm going to take myself off for a walk for a few hours until it's time to meet my colleague: I'll take loads of pictures for you, I promise.

Kisses from under the palm trees,

Stéphane

Dearest exile,

Tell me about this walk then: colourful streets, clear blue seas, lush vegetation? I need photos, details!

It's grey and horrible here – as usual. No magical tree has sprung up beside the Seine, and I haven't had time to go to the language school. The one thing I absolutely mustn't forget is to go and see Sylvia's solicitor; I've made an appointment for later in the week. It's the last thing I feel like doing.

I miss you.

Kisses from me and from Bourbaki too,

Hélène

Hawaii, 4 March (email)

Dear Hélène,

Sorry for my belated reply. Yesterday, I dozed off in the middle of writing the email I meant to send you. My excuse is that I gave my first seminar at the university, and my body's protesting at changing time zones so fast!

In reality, this 'paradise island' is a very strange place. Endless blue lagoons, plus palm trees, minus the Grand Hôtel des Thermes, honestly, you'd swear it was Saint-Malo ... right down to the temperature of the water, brrr. At times the wind is almost cold and you're shivering, and two minutes later you're boiling hot under a scorching sun. The proof that the biologist's ability to survive resides in the speed with which he adapts: I hurriedly went off to find the shop that sells those ghastly university baseball caps with huge visors that the students all wear. I bought one for you too; it'll wow everyone at your Parisian dinner parties.

On the other hand, I marvel at the vegetation. Here I'm able to observe specimens that I'd only seen in botanical gardens, or in photos. You'll say that's why

I've travelled eleven thousand kilometres, but it is strange to be able to touch plants that for me were mostly abstract images. I'm looking forward to the excursion to Big Island this weekend: another hour's flight, but I think it will be worth it. Be prepared to sit through endless slide shows during our long winter nights (which I sometimes find myself dreaming of, like the staid old Englishman I am at heart).

With love,

Stéphane

5 March (text message)

A goodnight kiss from here as you wake up there.
Thinking of you. Hélène.

5 March (text message)

Day here, night over there, I constantly see your face.
  Stéphane

Dear Stéphane,

It was so nice to hear your voice first thing this morning!
You'll have gathered Bourbaki was happy to hear from
you too from his enthusiastic meowing (though for the
sake of scientific objectivity, I must point out this cat
had not yet had his breakfast). I'm really glad the trip
is going well. But I'd be even gladder if it could hurry
up and finish.

Last night I went for a coffee after work with Boris,
the lecturer at INALCO, to hand him a copy of the
journal. I asked him to translate only the passages
pertaining to two people by the names of Nataliya
and Pierre, without going into any more detail. He
promised to call me in ten days or so to let me know
how he's getting on. I stayed on the café terrace after he
had gone and smoked a cigarillo, breaking all my good
resolutions. I felt strangely on edge, as if by showing
these pages to an outsider, I had thrown a boomerang
that would come back and hit me. I couldn't stand the
cold any longer and went home. I think it must be this

grey weather that's getting me down. Or being without my favourite lover. One or the other.

A thousand kisses,

H.

Dear Hélène,

Your favourite lover, as you call me (just you wait), is getting ready to board a Hawaii Airlines flight to visit the volcanoes on Big Island and risk his life (well, I'm exaggerating a little) to bring you back some magnificent photographs.

I'm joking, but I sensed a note of anxiety in your last email. I'm sorry to have burdened you with those documents before leaving. I should have waited until I was back, so as not to be so far away from you if you discover something that upsets you. We have already suffered that kind of situation. But from now on, we must tell ourselves, we're in this together.

I think I know where that last photo of your mother was taken. I'll tell you on my return from the island.

In the meantime, love and kisses,

Stéphane

PS I've racked my brains, but I simply can't figure out who the telephone number I saw in the diary belongs to.

And yet I'm convinced I used to know it by heart, and even dialled it when I was a child. It's really annoying me.

Dear Stéphane,

No news is good news, though given your current location, it wouldn't surprise me to hear you had no reception.

It's been quite a difficult day here. I went to see the solicitor straight after work: a very affable man, accompanied by a blushing intern looking awkward in his suit. My parents had clearly had their wills drawn up some time ago; everything has been left in good order, with no debts to pay. I'm to inherit the apartment on Rue de l'Observatoire, a number of bonds which will enable me to pay the inheritance tax, and a studio flat in Brittany. So here I am, a home-owner in Paris at going on for forty. As I listened to the will being read out, I pictured Sylvia with her slim glasses perched on the end of her nose, settling each item patiently and methodically, as was her way.

Her only stated wish was that if possible their shared library of books should not be dispersed. That was not my intention in any case. I am, however, going to try to find a way to have it moved from Rue de l'Observatoire.

I couldn't face living there without them, surrounded by memories ... Anyway, if you're ever in need of a Parisian pied-à-terre, from now on you'll be spoilt for choice.

Once he had finished reading, the solicitor told me he had something else he'd been keeping in trust for me: a small leather case Sylvia had given him three years earlier with instructions to pass it on to me after her death. The solicitor doesn't know what it contains; he put a lock and chain around it and has given me the key. Since I had nothing to carry it in, the intern handed me a plastic FNAC bag. I took the métro home with the bag on my lap, thinking what bizarre ways our parents have contrived to remember themselves to us. As I write, I haven't yet mustered the courage to open the case, which is still sitting on the kitchen counter. I'm beginning to be wary of the surprises our families have kept in store for us. Give me a ring when you can.

Thinking of you,

Hélène

Hawaii, 10 March (email)

Dearest,

Back safely from Big Island, it was magnificent. I'm exhausted. Will write again very soon.

Love and kisses,

Stéphane

Hawaii, 11 March (email)

Dearest Hélène,

I've only now managed to find the time to write to you, what with my teaching and recovering from the expedition to Big Island (extraordinary, breathtaking scenery). If you behave yourself, I'll bring you here one day. Despite the view over the car park and the plastic-wrapped pasteurised fruit, I'm beginning to find this place increasingly interesting. Earlier, on the campus, I picked a hibiscus flower off the grass and in my mind I put it in your hair. For a second I sensed your presence beside me, so real that it left me feeling perturbed.

While I understand your reticence, I'm burning with impatience to find out what the leather case the solicitor gave you contains: if I were in your shoes, I don't think I'd be able to stop myself from peeking inside, like a little boy dipping his finger in the jam jar. I'm willing to bet that it contains the explanation to everything you and I have been trying to understand over the last year. And that's what we hoped for from the start, isn't it?

Meanwhile, do you remember I told you that the photograph of your mother reminded me of a familiar setting? Now I know where it was taken: not far from Besançon. As a child I used to go for walks near that little chapel, sitting on my father's shoulders, or with my grandmother Séverine. There is now little doubt that our parents used to see each other, even though they were both married. But what I can't understand is how Nataliya came to be there: I find it hard to imagine Pierre bringing his woman friend (his mistress?) into his mother's house. Or maybe they were holed up in a nearby hotel, in secret? But why there rather than in Paris or Geneva? It's a mystery.

My colleagues are waiting for me to go and have dinner. That'll be all for today, my love.

Tender kisses,

Stéphane

Paris, 12 March (email)

Dear Stéphane,

You're right. Of course. And deep down, I want to know what's in it too. But I'm putting it off like a coward until Friday night, when the working week is over and I've had a chance to psych myself up for whatever I find.

You haven't said any more about the photos you had developed in London. What was on the film in the end?

Kisses, distant wanderer,

Hélène

Honolulu, 12 March (email)

Dear Hélène,

Nothing of great interest, just snowscapes. I'll show them to you when I'm back.

Love,

Stéphane

10

The photo is a faded Polaroid. The damaged, dog-eared edges and scratched surface show that the square of strong paper must have been handled many times. On the white bottom border, in tiny, squashed, sloping female handwriting, an inscription: 'Marsoulan, 1971'. The décor, with its arbour, ivy and the Etruscan mosaic on the lintel is familiar. The Zabvine family is gathered around a little girl sitting on her mother's knee. She is wearing a dress that must have been red, but which has faded to old rose in the photo. Her chubby legs are open, showing the bulge of her nappy. One of her hands is outstretched, proffering an unidentifiable object (liquorice stick, toy?); the other, raised vertically, is gently clasped in that of her mother, who must have been trying to hold her still.

The child's face is tilted slightly back to look at Nataliya, who is smiling at the camera. Despite the chromatic veil that has fallen over the image, the chestnut hair is noticeable, the mother's dark, the child's lighter, the shape of the face identical, the green eyes.

Their skin tone is emphasised by Nataliya's dress: with delicate pleats, in a blue that was originally turquoise, presumably, embroidered with different-coloured threads and golden beads, the hem ankle-length in defiance of the fashion of the day. Dressed thus, the young woman looks more Russian than ever. Her free hand is pressed against the little girl's stomach, gently supporting her, thus replicating the timeless image of that hybrid, shifting organic entity, the mother and daughter.

Behind them stands Daria, the first link in the chain of three generations, her hands clasped, imposing, but intimidated by the mechanical eye of the camera. Her Orthodox cross stands out clearly against the unbleached fabric of her embroidered blouse. Meanwhile Dr Zabvine is in a white shirt, tie and jacket; he is still wearing his doctor's coat over his clothes – a snatched moment of relaxation in the garden between appointments. His goatee and his spectacles make him look like a jovial Sigmund Freud. He is not touching Nataliya, out of a reticence that one senses is habitual in him, but he gazes at her and the child with tenderness, delighted to play the patriarch in his garden.

The only incongruity in this tableau, which despite everything has the hallmarks of a traditional family portrait, comes from the cat. Oleg has picked up the animal and slung it around his neck like a fur stole, its head and whiskers draped over one shoulder and its hind legs hanging down over the other, cupped in the doctor's hand. The cat, that inoffensive, affectionate mass that is, however, a reminder that any equilibrium exists only in the possibility that it might be destroyed.

Dear Stéphane,

Delighted that all is going well. It was late in your part of the world, but I couldn't resist hearing your voice. While I was looking through my window at the Paris sky, I could picture you over there in the warm rain you described.

I had a very different kind of phone call this evening, from Boris, the Russian lecturer, who told me he was about two-thirds of the way through the translation. From his tone of voice, I could tell something wasn't right. He kept asking if I knew the people mentioned in the diary, if they were still alive today. Anyway, he wants to talk to me in person before handing over what he's done; in fact he was very insistent about it. So he's going to drop in next Wednesday.

Still haven't worked up the courage to open the case. To take my mind off my cowardice, I decided to visit Rue de l'Observatoire to check everything was in order. The apartment has a sadness to it now, in a way it didn't while Sylvia was in hospital, a different kind of emptiness. I can't bear the thought of getting rid of all their things – dividing up some, selling the rest, and moving boxes and boxes of books.

I spent the whole evening there in the end, sitting on the floor of the library. Every so often, I detected Sylvia's perfume on the pages of a book she had held between her hands. She was the one who introduced me to Vicki Baum, believe it or not, and I found the series of 1960s paperback editions she used to pass on to me after she had finished them, with their slightly crisp pages and unmistakable smell. I had no idea she owned a first edition of Apollinaire's *Alcools* – it must be worth a fortune now.

An even more surprising find was a dog-eared copy of Nabokov's *Ada or Ardor* with notes scrawled in the margins and métro tickets and a restaurant bill shoved inside. I find it hard to believe Sylvia would treat a book so badly and even harder to imagine my father reading that kind of novel.

Michel's Bible was squeezed between two encyclopedias. Judging by the thick coating of dust on it, he can't have opened it very often these past few years. A black and white postcard used as a bookmark had been left inside. The picture showed a cluster of buildings, one of them with a little steeple, at the foot of a mountain ('Interlaken und die Jungfrau. 4,367m'). It was sent from Interlaken on 17 June 1970:

'My dear Michel. Getting lots of rest and enjoying the magnificent scenery. Maman told me Lena visited the zoo. With love, Nathalie.'

I sat there turning the little rectangle over in my hands – a piece of card my mother's hand had touched – tracing the beautifully neat handwriting with my fingertips. So here we are again, back where we began. What was she doing there, with her husband's full knowledge?

Tender kisses,

Hélène

Dearest Hélène,

I'm thinking of the way children play hunt-the-thimble: 'you're cold, warm, boiling'. For us adults it's more like: 'cold, warm, you're getting burnt'. Fear is not necessarily cowardice, Hélène.

We have fantasised so much about our parents, young, beautiful, imagining a love affair that was very romantic when all is said and done ... It is tempting to stop there and to hold on to the idyllic image of a couple under an arbour. Except that, if we run away from the past once again, I fear that sooner or later we'll be presented with the bill of unanswered questions, plus interest.

If you prefer, we can wait until I'm back. But perhaps your curiosity will get the better of you, and that will enable me to satisfy my own. I'm burning too, but to know, I think.

All my love,

Stéphane

Dear Stéphane,

I did it, I opened the case. Inside, I found a letter, from Sylvia, folded around another sealed envelope, along with two albums bound in blue morocco.

There they were, the photos of my mother I had never been allowed to see, painstakingly ordered, arranged and captioned in what must have been Sylvia's personal collection. She and Nataliya as little girls with plaits, and then as teenagers in the Saint-Serge days. A picture taken on a café terrace in which my mother is reading Nabokov (now everything's coming together) with a cigarette in her hand. One of your father with his arm around her neck as they queue for the cinema. The two of them on the beach, my mother's willowy frame vaguely resembling Catherine Pozzi, the poet (have you read her?). A photo from her wedding to Michel, too, taken at the top of the steps of Saint-Serge. He was a handsome man in his youth, my father, with his uniform and cap, and he was beaming with happiness that day; his young wife a little less so. And then a Polaroid picture of me, my mother and my grandparents. In a split second I could see myself back there, with the fat cat almost as big as me, the smell of lavender and ether when my grandfather kissed me and my mother's blue dress, *goluboye*: my memory of the word comes from there.

I didn't feel like delving any further. I was starting to wheeze again, a sign I should stop. Boris is coming this week and I still need to read Sylvia's long letter. I fell into bed without any dinner and slept for six hours straight, which hasn't happened in weeks. I only got up to write to you.

Loving thoughts,

Hélène

Dearest Hélène,

Part of me is sorry not to be with you at this time which I imagine is very unsettling; another feels it is probably better that this reunion should take place in private and solitude. How hard it must be to have to relearn that whole lexicon of childhood which was stolen from you. Mine was incomplete, but at least I know the people and the stages, and besides, I've always had the photos too.

I can't wait to be back. When I need some time to myself, I go to the park and memorise its fifty-five native species. I now know every heady or fetid fragrance by heart. No matter how far away we are, we still cling to our routines, the classes, seminars and lunches. And the nights go by, in the loneliness of my air-conditioned room, filled with nostalgia, emotion too, when I think what time it is in Paris.

You are particularly in my thoughts this evening.

Love,

Stéphane

Dear Stéphane,

I had a nightmare earlier. I was driving a car, even though I knew I didn't have a licence, and you were in the passenger seat. Before long, the road began to melt beneath us. You were making light of it, but I knew for certain we were going to die there, smothered in tar. I woke up covered in sweat.

So I got up, went into the kitchen, lit a cigarillo and opened Sylvia's letter.

I cried so much, the tears are still flowing now. I don't know how to say this ... We were right, at least broadly so, but we had missed many of the links of cause and effect. Now at least we can say there was a logic to what happened between our parents, if nothing more.

The worst of this is seeing just how wrong Sylvia and Michel got it, in their desperation to protect me at all costs. In that regard, the letter is like a switch in a dark room: everything, absolutely everything makes sense in light of its contents. I ask myself how they could have been so stupid. And yet I can't even bring myself to be angry with them.

I'll scan these pages for you now rather than await your return, since the letter concerns you as much as me and I expect you're eager to know what it says. I didn't like to open the other letter though. I don't know how it ended up there, but it's not addressed to me and I won't read it.

After I'd finished reading, I replayed every step of our journey in my mind, looking down from the window at the rear lights of the cars dancing silently in the Paris night. It's dawning on me that having immersed ourselves in the past, chasing after the shadows and mysteries of other people's lives, time is suddenly pushing us onwards, together, relentlessly. And it will snuff us out too, when our turn comes. Stéphane, *dorogoy*, who will remember us when we're gone?

But for now, the question I ask above all others is what you're going to think of them.

Hélène

My dear Hélène,

By the time you read these words I will have departed this world. First and foremost I want you to know how much your father and I loved you, and I hope you never doubt it. You have been our ray of sunshine, bringing us joy and, later, such pride. Life dealt me a cruel hand in not giving me children, but it made amends by allowing me to be a mother to you. When I look at you now and the person you have become – so generous and sweet-natured – I tell myself yes, we made a lot of mistakes, but at least we succeeded in surrounding you with the love you so deserved. You know I don't believe in the hereafter, yet a little part of me hopes that wherever I end up, I will be with your father again and together we can continue to watch over you.

It has been two weeks since the doctor told me I am suffering from Alzheimer's, but I had seen it coming a long way off; there were too many holes in my memory, too many muddles. I've read up on it and I know what's going to happen: I will begin to forget, first the recent past, then more distant memories. There may come a day when I am no longer able to recognise you. Naturally I hope my lungs will have carried me off before then, but I have to consider all the practical consequences now.

There is one thing I want to do before I go and while my memory is still intact — at least, those memories that concern you. Something I should have done long ago, but I lacked the courage. And I don't know how to broach the subject with you now; I can't bear the thought of throwing you off balance or making you unhappy. But neither can I stomach the prospect of taking this secret with me to the grave, leaving you to inherit nothing but unanswered questions.

My solicitor will hand this letter to you after my death. It's a convenient solution — too convenient, perhaps, but at least it means you can choose when to read it and put it aside if you don't feel ready yet. I want to tell you about your mother, Hélène — your mother, Nataliya Zabvina, who died soon after you turned four and about whom we have hidden the full truth from you. You will find two albums inside this box filled with photos of her and me, along with the last letter sent by someone very dear to her. She never got the chance to read it. It's for you to decide what to do with it.

I'm ashamed to think of all the times you came to me with your sweet little face, asking questions which I systematically avoided answering. But you must understand, your father didn't want us to talk about your mother and I was afraid of opening up old wounds which had taken years to heal. I say 'you must understand', but in fact you're perfectly entitled not to understand, to hate me even. What we did, holding back the truth for so long, was wrong, deeply wrong, and I'm all too aware of it.

Your mother, Nataliya (whom we called Natasha) and I were childhood friends. Her parents had come over from Russia at the end of the war; her father was enlisted in the Germans' forced labour programme and feared reprisals should he return. Before the war in St Petersburg — or Leningrad as it was then called — he had been a brilliant and highly regarded young doctor and had even published a short paper on paediatric ophthalmology. Afterwards, he was merely a wretched exile like so many others in Europe who had lost everything. But he thanked God he had escaped with his life.

In 1947 he managed to get his wife, Daria, and their daughter out of Austria (where they had fled at the end of the war) via Germany to join him in Paris. The first thing he did was get a job in a factory to feed himself and his family. Due to medical council red tape, he had to re-sit some of his exams at the university in Paris, and it wasn't until late in 1953 that he was finally given approval to practise again. He opened a small surgery on Rue de la Mouzaïa where he was mainly a general practitioner, and transferred to the 12th *arrondissement* as soon as he was able. Before long he had built up a patient base there, this time practising his specialism. The move had symbolic significance for him: a fresh start in a slightly smarter neighbourhood where he was no longer the humble factory worker returning to medicine, but the venerable Dr Zabvine, ophthalmologist. He mostly treated children; his young patients adored him for his humour and Russian accent, and their mothers were won over by his old-fashioned manners. It's true he was a very funny man, always playing pranks on his wife such as swapping the flour for icing sugar or pretending to listen to the chicken's heartbeat before carving it. Religion was almost the only thing he never joked about.

Natasha, then, arrived at the same time as her mother, not quite two years after the war had ended. She was six years old at the time, and didn't speak a word of French. I met her a few years later, in the penultimate year of primary school, when we sat together in class. Since my parents, who had emigrated before the war, had taught me Russian at home, we soon began conversing in the language and quickly became inseparable. You wouldn't believe how often we were scolded! Writing lines of 'I must not chatter in Russian during mathematics lessons' was our daily punishment. Not only that, but Natasha was even worse than Oleg; if ever there was a chance to be silly, she leapt at it. Once or twice we were called names like Russki, or told to go back where we came from, but overall my memories of that time are happy ones, the whole gang of us hurtling crazily down Rue de la Mouzaïa on our old bicycles.

Your mother loved music and had a very pretty

voice. Her father scrimped and saved to pay for lessons with a Russian émigré pianist even worse off than he was. Your grandmother who, like many refugees, had become very devout in exile, enrolled Natasha in the parish choir of Saint-Serge in the 19th *arrondissement*. It was there that your mother met the boy who went on to become her closest friend. His name is, or was – I don't know if he's still alive – Jean Pamiat. He came from a family of White Russians who had emigrated in 1917. Jean was an incredible character, always dressed like an aristocrat despite not having a *sou* to his name. He had just come back from military service – he was older than us – and was working around the Buttes-Chaumont as a photographer's apprentice. He would have us all in stitches with his impressions of the rector of Saint-Serge; he only came to church for the music. It was a funny time, you know. Some of the kids really didn't have much; they would wear their fathers' old suit jackets and shoes with holes in them, and had no concept of what a holiday meant. But at the same time, when I think back to my childhood, my memory is of a lost paradise.

Natasha and I remained friends throughout secondary school and we sat the baccalauréat in the same year; she specialised in philosophy while I took maths. We were closer than ever. I was very fashion-conscious and always dressed up to the nines (you know me); she would walk about with one sleeve twisted, her collar sticking up and her hair all over the place, as though her body wouldn't let her clothes have the last word. Yet there was something irresistible about her. She had all the boys falling at her feet and she didn't even notice, because all she cared about was music. I should have been jealous, but it was impossible to hold anything against her for more than three seconds because her wit (which could be ferocious) and generosity were so infectious. She was one of those people born with a kind of light inside them, drawing us to them in awe and wonder.

Both of us passed the *bac* with good grades, and I had my first hangover after the little party Oleg and my father threw in our honour, both of them bursting with pride. That same year the Zabvines moved house, but as we had both enrolled at the Sorbonne – Natasha to study English and I history – we still saw a lot of each other. Books were expensive in those days, so we both did a bit of teaching to make ends meet. The one luxury we allowed ourselves was a daily copy of *Le Monde*; we would separate the pages and take turns reading them. Occasionally we would stop off at a bar on our way home from Sainte-Geneviève library, sipping our café crèmes and sharing our dreams for the future. I wanted to teach history, whereas Natasha had plans to become a psychoanalyst or a novelist. That was what marked us out from most girls of our age, and the main reason we got on so well: we were nonconformists. We had no desire to get married and end up like our friends' sisters, with three children by the age of thirty and a life divided between shopping, washing-up and laundry. This didn't always make us very popular with the boys.

Midway through our first or second term, I can't remember precisely, Natasha began to change. She became moody, distant, suffering spells of gloom that were very unlike her. I kept asking what was wrong until she finally admitted that Jean Pamiat had introduced her to one of his army friends, a photographer, and she hadn't stopped thinking about him since. She was losing sleep over it and could barely eat.

So, feeling very pleased with myself, I did what good friends do: I went to persuade Jean to set up a date between this young man, whose name was Pierre, and your mother. They fell, as the saying goes, head over heels in love, and were engaged within two months. I have rarely seen two people so strikingly well matched. They were like two faces of the same being – just seeing them walk down the road together brought a lump to your throat, and they turned heads wherever they went. The Zabvines, on the other hand, were rather less enchanted. Firstly, because Pierre was eight years older than your mother; and secondly, because he did not have what we would nowadays call a 'stable income', and was living off photographic commissions and odd jobs. It had been such a struggle for Oleg to lift his family out of relative poverty that he could not bear to hand his daughter over to an impoverished 'artist'. But what Daria could not forgive Pierre was his agnosticism and irreverence towards all forms of religion, which he saw as an insult to human intelligence. She had caught him quoting one or two of Voltaire's anti-religious jibes, which did not go down well at all.

And so, after almost a year, your grandparents made Natasha break off the engagement. Such a statement must sound ridiculous to a woman of your generation, but it wasn't for ours, I can assure you. We were still minors until the age of twenty-one and getting married without permission was out of the question. On top of that, Natasha had no money, had not finished her studies, and the Zabvines had threatened to cut her off; Pierre, meanwhile, was already on the breadline. In my opinion, if the Zabvines had felt they had no choice in the matter, they might have backed down, but there you are. The real problem was that Natasha adored her parents and they her, and she chose to suffer rather than cause them pain. And so it was with the heaviest of hearts that she agreed to leave her fiancé. Poor thing, she cried so many tears that year; poor things, I should say, because it was a terrible time for Pierre too. I know he begged her to change her mind, and went to see Oleg too, but nothing could persuade your grandparents to go back on their decision.

Afterwards, Natasha never quite regained the joie de vivre I knew and loved; it was as if part of her had been shut off and she had suddenly aged by several years. She fooled around less, instead making cruel sarcastic remarks which were completely out of character. For several years, she refused to set foot in a concert hall; she couldn't bear to hear a single note without Pierre, with whom she had so enjoyed listening to music. In spite of everything, he had asked her to keep the engagement ring and she continued to wear it on a chain around her neck. Soon after she broke off their engagement, Pierre left Paris for Switzerland. When she found out, Tasha was despondent, because of course she still loved him. She just about managed to finish her degree, after I had badgered her to turn up for her exams. She scraped a pass, with much lower marks than she deserved, and then looked for work. It was around that time we began to drift apart.

She found a job through one of Oleg's patients, a lawyer who needed an English-speaking secretary. She was still living with her parents, not far from Cours de Vincennes. We sometimes went to the pictures together on the few evenings I took off from revising for my teaching exams. Once or twice she brought someone with her, a nice boy called Vladimir or Vasily or something, but he wasn't on the scene for very long. I don't think she had got over her broken heart. We no longer saw Jean Pamiat, who had also left for Switzerland, but he wrote to us. I heard – from him, I suppose – that Pierre had got married two years after the engagement was broken off and had a little boy. I never told Natasha.

She had become quite secretive herself. Her lawyer boss had ended up asking her to marry him, but she turned him down, much to her parents' displeasure. I had failed my teaching exams and while weighing up whether or not to enrol for a PhD in history, I took a job at the Bibliothèque Nationale to tide me over. I ended up staying there for the rest of my career, and I think I was happier than I would have been teaching a class of teenagers. At that point, I was only seeing Natasha every three or four months; I had started going out with one of the librarians at work, and we ended up getting married in 1963. Your mother and Jean were my witnesses.

Sadly, my husband, who was also called Jean, died two years later from a poorly treated collapsed lung. I was devastated, as you can imagine – it was all so sudden. Had it not been for Natasha, I think I might have done something stupid. She supported me, kept me company, even came to live in our apartment for a few months so she could make sure I was eating and help me through my grief. Things slowly got back to some kind of normality. The years went by and I carried on living the life of a young widow. Natasha in her mid-twenties was still 'on the shelf', as they say; being unmarried at that age was cause for concern in those days. After refusing the lawyer's proposal, she changed jobs and was now employed by a publisher, compiling English grammar textbooks. She enjoyed her work. She had moved out of her parents' home and was living in a little studio near the Jussieu campus. We used to rent a house in Brittany together for a week every year. One summer, she confided she was afraid of what the future held, and that her parents were driving her up the wall saying she was going to end up an old maid.

A few months after that, she told me she was engaged to a young doctor, Michel Hivert. She introduced me to him a week later. He was Breton, shy, very intelligent and rather mysterious, and he was just finishing his training at the École de Santé des Armées. I think he must have met the Zabvines through a work do while he was completing his internship at Val-de-Grâce military hospital. The old doctor had taken the young man under his wing as a kind of spiritual son. The fact he was a practising Catholic, if not Russian Orthodox, went down well with Daria, and I suspect it was the parents who arranged the engagement. In any case, it was clear to me that Natasha's feelings for this young man were nothing compared to the passion she had felt for Pierre. Michel, on the other hand, was besotted with Natasha, who was both beautiful and cultured, and he treated her as if she were a goddess. Sometimes the three of us would go out to a café and he wouldn't say a word all evening but simply stare longingly at her, leaving me feeling somewhat uncomfortable.

Perhaps I shouldn't be telling you this, but if Michel was in love, for Nataliya it was more what might be termed a marriage of convenience, entered into for the sake of form. Again, you must remember that in those days such things happened all the time and, for a woman, being single was treated like an affliction. Sometimes, these orchestrated unions produced couples who held each other in mutual regard and managed to build a stable life together. I have always wondered what would have happened had May '68 come a few months sooner, or Natasha been allowed to marry Pierre. But events took a different course, and it was Michel Hivert who led her down the aisle in February '68. They went to great lengths to be granted an Orthodox ceremony. It was probably the happiest day of Daria's life, watching her daughter get married at Saint-Serge. Jean Pamiat and I were witnesses (he wore a silk suit), Michel's fellow students were there in full dress uniform and the choir sang beautifully. Afterwards there was a huge party where we all drank each other under the table — even Daria, who started singing 'Kalinka' at the top of her voice. You should have seen the faces of the Breton contingent! Your father destroyed his wedding photographs but I kept the one I took, and I've never forgotten the trace of melancholy on Natasha's face. The icon of happiness was cracked from the beginning and the signs were there, right before our eyes. But we chose not to see them.

Hawaii, 17 March (email)

Dearest Hélène,

Here I am on my balcony at the other end of the earth, and I'm looking at the photo of your parents' wedding, which I've got up on screen. You look so very much like your mother. I stopped midway through reading the letter with a lump in my throat. I can imagine how distraught Pierre and Natasha must have been to be separated, and I want to take a moment to find a place where my thoughts can be with you, see your face again, your hands as you pour water to make tea or grope for your glasses, the way you converse with your cat or run your hands through my hair. All the delicious and intense things I feel when I'm with you, beside you, close to you. Because *we* are alive.

And like you, I am looking back giddily over this year of seeking, which came and shattered the routine of my quiet – probably too quiet – life. When I first wrote to you, I thought, rather presumptuously, that my reply was simply a noble gesture to calm the anxiety and answer the questions of an unknown correspondent. By the time we had exchanged three letters, things had changed dramatically. The unease you described in your struggle with this silent past was, word for word, my own.

Our quest has given me the opportunity to understand the things that can break the life of a man, my father; to make sense of that extinction of his person that we witnessed, powerless to help. From one season to the next, and, above all, looking through the albums, I was discovering Pierre, the energy he invested in capturing on film the heartrending light of empty spaces. I guessed that these images were for him the representations of private aspirations, and that even aside from seeking refuge from his unhappy marriage, he was someone who craved solitude. I understand now how the separation of 1960 was certainly one of the sources of that pain, which he never expressed other than through photographs.

You ask who will remember us. I'd gladly tell you that first of all, it's up to us to reinvent a present that will be ours, one that the dead cannot take away from us. We are driven forward, it's true. But side by side this time.

Stéphane

11

The snowflakes have settled, carpeting the ground and enveloping everything – the earth, trees and paths – in a soft blanket of pure white. No footsteps have disturbed the virgin surface, and, if they did, they would produce that muffled, crunching sound of snow being trampled. The outlines of the yews, pines and larches are lost under swollen tunics that weigh heavily on their sturdy branches. It is one of those wan January mornings when the freezing air bites your fingers and face and seeps up your legs. One of those mornings when winter like a silversmith has rimed the tiniest protuberance, stone, railings and bars, and snow has blanketed the chaos of the world with its fragile molecular cathedrals.

Apart from a few frozen birds, the animals have abandoned the place, which is too wild to be a clearing or a field, too open to shelter creatures or homes.

There are curious, slightly fuzzy, vertical shapes dotted around and it takes a moment to realise what they are. The photographer, who failed to produce a clear image, lighted on a large snowy mass measuring one and a half metres by three. The layer of snow conceals a rectangular tomb, softening its irregular contours and sharp edges. The uniformity of the whitish blanket is broken in only two places. On one side, a prominent stem pokes up, the ghost of a bunch of flowers invisible under the snow: the drop of blood of a frozen rose. At the other end is the recognisable shape of the three-beamed Orthodox cross, the lowest beam slanting, departing from the usual perpendicular geometry of cemeteries.

Sylvia's Letter (2)

Not long after the wedding, having graduated, your father received his first posting. He and Natasha moved to Brest, where his garrison was stationed. She wrote to me from time to time and sent the occasional postcard. She seemed bored whenever Michel was away, as he was most of the time. He had forbidden her to work, out of principle, and besides she had fallen pregnant straight away. He had, however, bought her a piano on hire purchase to give her something to occupy her time. She told me she would spend whole days sight-reading and playing Chopin waltzes.

You were born prematurely at seven and a half months after a difficult labour, and we were worried you might not survive. You had to stay in hospital for four months while Natasha slowly recovered from a pulmonary embolism, but in the end you both pulled through. Your grandmother rushed over to see you as soon as you were born and prayed for you from dawn until dusk, took care of you and showered you with love. It really was touch and go for a while. She had got it into her head to call you Hélène Seryozha

Hivert – the masculine diminutive of Sergey, which she wanted to try to pass off as a girl's name! But neither the council nor the Catholic priest would register it, and I don't think Michel put up much of a fight.

Your mother asked me to be your godmother, and I was honoured to accept: you'll find the christening notice among the other papers.

Judging by Tasha's letters, things seemed to pick up around then. She sounded happy: she adored you, her Lena, her Lenochka, her little princess. When you were about nine months old, she began bringing you to Paris when Michel was away; he could no longer put off resuming his assignments overseas. To your grandparents, you were something approaching the eighth wonder of the world ... Oleg and Daria had decided to teach you Russian, which your mother already spoke to you when her husband wasn't around. Your grandmother even tried to take you to vespers at Saint-Serge once, but apparently you made so much noise she never did it again!

I often dropped in to Rue Marsoulan, so I saw quite a bit of you. You were absolutely adorable, babbling away and trying to attract the attention of the cat, a fat tomcat who was shut away every night for fear he might lie on top of you and suffocate you. For your first birthday, I bought you a wooden toy with animals painted on it, and I remember telling you their names in Russian. I think *kot* was your first word when you started talking.

I came to see you in Brest, too – your parents invited me one Christmas. The flat was gloomy and the town, which had been completely rebuilt after the war, was also quite depressing. Michel and Nataliya – whom he called 'Nathalie' – were getting on well, but even so it always seemed to me there was something about them as a couple that didn't quite work. Natasha, who was usually so talkative, would just sit there with a fixed, distracted smile plastered across her face whenever her husband was in the room. This pleasant yet vaguely distant demeanour served as a kind of defence mechanism, but it was clear that something was wrong beneath the veneer. I don't think there was much love lost between her and her in-laws, Breton traditionalists who still hadn't resigned themselves to Michel having married 'the Russian girl'. In Brest, your mother was getting better and better at the piano, and she had a few friends, mostly officers' wives. But they never became close: her glorious untidiness, her chain-smoking (always Craven As), lack of interest in baby talk and increasingly staunch feminism made her stand out. Too much.

She still wasn't working. The only remnant of her past life – music aside – was her passion for reading, which remained as fervent as ever. More than once I witnessed her ignoring your cries until she had finished her chapter. She told me she even read while she was breastfeeding you! One night while I was staying with you, I found her fast asleep on the sofa with a book, even though Michel had returned from his posting. She was still there the next morning. I don't think it was a one-off.

It was September 1970, I remember well, when I received a letter from Natasha asking to see me as soon as possible. She came to Paris, leaving you behind, and I met her in a café near the Odéon. She told me she had seen Pierre, her fiancé of 1960, again; she had bumped into him by chance while on holiday in Switzerland, and was having an affair with him. Then, Hélène, I did something I'm still ashamed of to this day: I lectured her. In no uncertain terms. I told her she had lost her mind, that she must break it off at once, think of her family, think of you. I called her a bad daughter, an unfit mother and who knows what other foolish things besides. You see, I had lost my husband; Jean and I hadn't had the chance to have children, and I was lonely, pretty unhappy and probably rather bitter. In the end I was so angry I called her *sumasshedshaya* – crazy, reckless. I don't think she expected me to react the way I did. She blanched, gathered up her things, paid for her coffee and left. That was the last time I saw her alive.

I've replayed that scene over and over in my head hundreds of times since. I would give anything for it not to have happened but it did, and there's nothing I can do about it. The following year, Natasha sent me a card from Saint-Malo, and another one to wish me a happy New Year. I felt so awkward about the way I had reacted, yet unable to get down off my high horse, and I didn't know what to write back. So I didn't. Then, a little over two years after we had last spoken, she called me at work one October evening, from a café. She told me something serious had happened and she was taking the train to see Jean in Geneva. She sounded awful; I think she was in tears. She asked me to look after you should anything happen and then she hung up, saying she would call me back.

A few days later, I received a letter from Michel Hivert with another letter addressed to Natasha inside. I don't know how he had worked out that I knew where she was; perhaps he simply guessed. I duly forwarded it, and took the opportunity to ask how she was. But Natasha still didn't call me back. So, after going to great pains to track down Jean's telephone number (there was no internet back then, of course), I called from the post office to find out what was going on. International telephone calls were prohibitively expensive, so I had to be brief. Jean told me Natasha had left her husband and was not in the best shape, but he was looking after her. I could tell they were hiding something from me. They no longer trusted me and, in a way, it was my own fault.

On the evening of 18 November, Jean sent me a telegram telling me to come to a town called Pontarlier in the Jura, and to bring the Zabvines with me. Your mother had been involved in a car accident. We set off in the early hours of the next morning, but by the time we arrived, after a long day driving through rain and snow, it was too late. Tasha had sustained serious head injuries and a perforated lung, and she died without regaining consciousness. I always told you she was cremated, but that wasn't true; she was buried initially at the cemetery in Pontarlier because the terrible weather had made the roads impassable. Then, four months later, her body was moved to the cemetery at Thiais just outside Paris, on the express wishes of the Zabvines. She was laid to rest in the Orthodox section; you can find her grave and say a prayer for her there, if you wish. Your grandparents are buried there too.

We were all there in Pontarlier. All except your father, who had been posted to a remote part of New Caledonia. He was informed too late to catch a flight in time, and arrived twenty-four hours after the funeral. He never forgave himself for that, among many other things.

The police report concluded it was an accident. The roads were icy, there was thick fog and Natasha was travelling in Jean's car, which she can't have been used to driving. I don't know what she was doing there or where she was going, but I promise you it was an accident, a tragic accident. There's no doubt about that.

I wanted to come and see you on my way back home so I took the train to Brest, but your father wouldn't allow me in. He was devastated, and angry too. I think he had found out about the affair and thought I was in on the secret. I told myself he was in shock, that he just needed time, and I resolved to come back when things had calmed down.

But when I next tried to get in touch in early 1973, he had moved house without leaving a forwarding address. I did all I could to locate you, to no avail. Your grandparents hadn't heard anything either and were at their wits' end. They were tearing their hair out, absolutely desperate to see you. Despite serious misgivings, your grandfather ended up hiring a private detective, but two months later he had a heart attack and died; the detective took the money and ran. My own attempts at finding you remained fruitless; it was as if you had vanished into thin air. Then, three years later, I happened to overhear a conversation in a waiting room: a woman was talking about her son, a soldier who had suffered an eye injury operated on by 'Dr Hivert'. It could only be your father. I asked the woman where he practised, rang his surgery at Val-de-Grâce hospital and he agreed to speak to me. A few days later, I was able to see you again.

You had grown so much! You were now seven years old and when you walked into the room, it brought tears to my eyes. You were Tasha in miniature. You had (and still have) exactly the same smile, the same unruly hair (and a skew-whiff velvet bow), the same expression. You inherited her beauty, you know. But what struck me most, there and then, was how sad you looked. You never smiled but only gazed around you with those big pale eyes, not saying a word. You didn't recognise me, of course, and I didn't even dare kiss you for fear of frightening you. Your father explained that you had not spoken at home or school for several months and he had had to ask his psychiatrist colleagues to step in to prevent you from being moved to a special school, since autism had been mentioned. It turned out you had only been back in Paris a few weeks: to begin with, Michel had left you with his parents, your paternal grandparents. He obtained a transfer to Marseille and came to fetch you to live with him, and then the pair of you went to Polynesia for a long-term posting. But while you were there, you picked up a quite serious flu-like virus called dengue fever, and it took you a long time to get over it. He sent you back to France to be looked after by one of his sisters, who lived near Le Mans, until he could get a posting back home. It was at that point you stopped talking.

I think you had been through too much upheaval and your silence was your way of saying you had had enough. Your father was raising you on his own in Paris, with a little help from his other sister, Madeleine, but his work was very demanding, and he was losing patience with your refusal to speak. If he agreed to let you spend time with me, it's because he would have agreed to anything that might help you get better. He even told me he wouldn't mind you seeing your grandmother again; what he didn't know was that Daria had died of cancer the previous year.

So I was able to spend some time with you, taking you

to the zoo at Vincennes, ice-skating and to the cinema. You were a lovely child, good as gold; you looked around, taking everything in. But you never asked for anything; never said anything at all.

Even so, it didn't take long to work out that there were some things you liked more than others: the overground sections of the métro (you would stare out of the window with both hands pressed against the glass); the stuffed animals at the natural history museum; hot chocolate; the piano, which I played with your little squirrel-like hands resting on top of mine. Sometimes when you were with me on a Sunday, you fell asleep in my arms sucking your thumb like a baby, and I would rock you to the Russian nursery rhymes your mother used to sing to you. You were so avid for affection, and I became more attached to you each day.

One evening on the métro, enthralled by the sight of the winter lights twinkling over the Seine, you grabbed hold of my sleeve and said 'Sylvia'. It was the first word I had heard you utter since your return and I squeezed you so tightly you squirmed to be let go. You were so unused to the sound of your own voice that afterwards you became overexcited and couldn't stop shouting 'Syl-via, Syl-via' as we walked through the underground tunnels while I mimed applause, beaming with delight. People turned and stared at us as if we were completely mad. Yet the first time you said 'pa-pa' to Michel again, he turned away to hide the emotion on his face. Your silence had been a living nightmare for him.

From then on, your father began to relax a little. He invited me round for dinner with you. Then he came with us to the zoo. And soon the three of us were doing lots of things together, especially going to concerts, because you loved music and could sit still for hours listening to Chopin. You gradually became more comfortable in your own skin. For your eighth birthday, with Michel's consent, I bought you a kitten, the kitten who would grow to become our big fat Chacha. It was the first time I had seen you really laugh; you seemed so delighted with your present. When I asked what you wanted to call it, you immediately replied 'Koshka'. Michel pursed his lips and told you a French name would be nicer. You never said it again in front of him, but I know you carried on calling your cat the name you had chosen. You still didn't say much to us, but I sometimes heard you in your bedroom holding forth to the animal in a made-up language I could make neither head nor tail of. You seemed to be progressing all the time. And within a few weeks, you were talking to us again.

Two years later, in 1978, Michel asked me to marry him. The idea of me marrying my best friend's husband, and he his dead wife's best friend, will no doubt seem peculiar to you. But your father and I had a great deal in common: in spite of his military background, he was a scholarly man, one of the old breed of medics interested in botany and poetry, and I worked in the book world. We both enjoyed music as well as peace and quiet. And above all, we both loved you. One night, when he had drunk too much whisky and the past must have been weighing more heavily on him than usual, Michel confessed that he had thrown your mother out a few weeks before the accident. At the time, he was religious, and madly in love with her, and he reacted very, very badly to the news of her affair. Not a world away from how I had behaved myself. You cannot imagine how guilty he felt. He never spoke of it again, but his nightmares gave him away: he would wake up gasping, covered in sweat, and go out walking the streets in the middle of the night. I sometimes didn't see him again until breakfast, by which time I would be frantic, worrying he was never coming back.

I know you sometimes felt he was distant or irritable with you, and you're right. But it wasn't his fault; you reminded him so much of Natasha, it was hard for him even to cuddle you or look at you. What's more, he was consumed with guilt, blaming himself (quite wrongly, in my opinion) for the accident that deprived you of your mother. Through no fault of yours, he felt your very presence as a silent rebuke against what he believed to be his own worst actions. Some days, it was too much for him to bear.

As for me, I had Natasha's last words going round in my head and was haunted by the knowledge that I had pushed her away when she most needed me. She had asked me to take care of you, and you were now half-orphaned. On a more selfish note, my loneliness was becoming harder to bear, time was passing and my biological clock – as it's called nowadays – was ticking. I wanted someone to come home to, a companion, and for you to be my little girl. So I agreed to marry your father on one condition: that I be allowed legally to adopt you. The papers were signed the following year. Michel also laid down two preconditions: we would never talk about your mother and I was never to address you in Russian. I kept my side of the bargain too. You must think us monstrous and calculating, and no doubt it was our sense of guilt that inspired the vain hope that blocking out the past might make the pain go away. But I promise you we both sincerely believed it was the best thing to do for your sake. And when, a decade or so later, I began to wonder if we'd got it wrong, it was too late to go back without accepting the prospect of you turning against us and pushing us away. We weren't willing to take that risk.

You know what happened next: our life together, the three of us. It wasn't all bad, I don't think. Yes, your father still had the odd temper, and he never came to terms with Natasha's death. But he had 'started over', as the expression goes, and firmly closed the lid on the past. He had distanced himself from his parents, who for all their devoutness never took the slightest interest in you. He, on the other hand, had turned his back on religion entirely. Yet he continued to visit Thiais every 19 November to lay flowers on Natasha's grave, and I would go with him. I took you there once without telling him, one spring afternoon when you were eight. I couldn't tell you why. I just wanted you to be near one another, at least once. The last time I made the trip with Michel, when his health was beginning to fail, we passed an old man, tall but frail, walking back along the path through the cemetery on the arm of a younger man the spitting image of him at the same age. It was Pierre Crüsten. He didn't recognise me. It had been thirty years, after all.

Time passed happily enough for us, in spite of your low periods and recurring nightmares about accidents. You were our daughter, the most adorable child, and you always remained so, even when you were fifteen and dyed your hair green, your bedroom reeked of cigarettes smoked in secret and you called us 'a pair of old right-wing reactionaries' (your words exactly!) for not letting you go to the cinema on school nights. And in the end you grew into the beautiful person you are today.

In 1973, I had received a card from Jean Pamiat, who had left his job at the newspaper to set up a small commercial photography studio in Lausanne. Things seemed to be going well for him, and we saw each other three or four times over the next few years, whenever he was in Paris. But the weight of Natasha's memory hung heavy between us and we stopped meeting once I was back in touch with you and Michel. I suppose this tacit split was a way of severing the one remaining link with the past, and thereby protecting you from it.

If only it were that easy. For your fifteenth birthday, you had your heart set on a camera. At first we tried to tell ourselves it was a passing craze, but once we saw how much time you were spending developing pictures up in the attic room, it was clear you really had a passion for it. Then you announced you were going to write your master's dissertation on family photo albums in literature, and it seemed to me we were seeing the first cracks appearing in our wall of silence. And when you took up Russian seven years ago, Michel and I understood that all the outward calm had been deceptive; you had never stopped questioning where you came from, trying to find the part of you that was missing. You had an incredible instinct for unearthing your history, in spite of the fact we had erased all the material clues that might have shown you the way. Repeatedly failing your driving test, as if afraid of replicating your mother's fate, was the most obvious example. I also sensed the sadness we had striven to ward off rearing its ugly head once more. Many years later you told me that the idea of having children terrified you and that you had just left Hervé, who was desperate to have them, for that very reason. That was when the scope and depth of our mistake really sank in. I was on the verge of telling you everything when your father fell ill. I had no choice but to give him my undivided attention.

I have no idea whether all that I have written will help you to see things more clearly. But I have every faith in you. Like Natasha, you are drawn to the light, and we have done nothing but surround you in shadows. It may be late in the day, but I am urging you now to brush those shadows aside, to find the strength never to let them descend on you again. I don't know what you will think of us now that you know the truth. You might hate us for all the lies we told, and if so, I would understand. But I'm old enough to know that hatred is a poison that harms the person who feels it the most; something Michel learned through bitter experience. Even if you cannot bring yourself to forgive us just yet, please keep a place in your heart for the three of us – your mother, your father and me. And more than anything, try to remember that everything we have done, even the things we did wrong – especially those – we did out of love for you, *solnyshko*.

Be happy, my darling Hélène.

I love you with all my heart.

Sylvia Hivert

Dear Hélène,

It was immediately clear to me from your letter that the woman who brought you up was an exceptional person. Mistakes, clumsiness, I grant you. But what love in those silences, in those ridiculous efforts whose hopelessness she herself realised. The simple fact that she had the courage to write you that letter is a mark of extraordinary affection.

I too owe her a great deal, indirectly. How would I have known, otherwise? Reading about my father's past, the past I was unaware of, was deeply upsetting but also reassuring, in a way. I have always been convinced, even though I found it hard to explain, that he had two different personalities. This account touches on his other side, the one that Philippe and I glimpsed only briefly: that of a free man, an adventurer, passionate about his art, a man in love, the man in the portrait of 1971. There's something cruel in the thought that we, his family, represented the flipside of that life, but what can we do other than accept it now?

After Natasha's death, he must have grieved for her

and, worse, grieved without being able to talk about it, which is appalling. Now I understand why he avoided us as he did, why he found it so hard to bear the presence of others. He must have wanted to shut himself away with his sorrow, ultimately the only thing that remained of her.

It was your mother he went to see in Thiais cemetery, I'm certain of it. And I bumped into your parents, that day, even though I don't remember them. When Pierre and I were already on our way back to Geneva, you must have been waiting somewhere for them. Our destinies, yours and mine, could have so easily continued unaware of each other, dearest Hélène. I find that retrospective thought almost unbearable.

I am with you, more than ever.

Stéphane

Paris, 18 March (email)

Dear Stéphane,

For my part, after all that time desperately seeking the truth – searching, questioning, poring over albums – I'm left with an overwhelming feeling of emptiness. Is that really it? Can a life be summed up in the dozen pages of a letter? Thirty years of censorship overturned by 110 photos in an album? I will never know any more about Nataliya Zabvina, unless Jean's diary brings some revelation to light. But at this stage, I can't imagine what it could tell us that we don't already know. I feel all at sea tonight. The thought of you is practically the only light shining through these murky waters.

Hélène

Hawaii, 18 March (email)

Hélène,

In three days I'll be home. And if you come to England, in four, we'll be together.

Stéphane

Paris, 19 March (email)

I'll be at Heathrow, waiting for you.

H.

I've come back to the computer because on my return from the museum this evening I had a visit from Boris, the Russian lecturer. He had come to give me the translation. We had coffee together in the kitchen. He couldn't stop squirming on his stool and he asked me again if I knew the people mentioned in the diary. When I told him, as I had Vera, 'Ya doch Natalii Zabviny,' the colour drained from his face and he said, 'Then you must not read it.' He said the diary tells of unhappy events I am better off not knowing about; I reassured him that we were already aware of the essence of it. Boris stayed for dinner and, with the bundle of paper sitting on the counter within arm's reach, we had a long conversation about secrets. I tried to explain how hard it had been for you and me, and why we were both so keen to try to piece together the story of what happened. Boris, who had a grandfather caught up in some denunciation scandal, told me that contrary to what you might think, in most cases the truth is crueller than anything you had imagined. He said, 'You know, afterwards, you won't be able to get it out of your head.' On his way out, he tried to give me back my cheque and take the translation and diary with him, to 'shelter' me from them. I refused on both counts.

Even so, I'm not sure I want to read it. It's too late, anyway; everyone involved is dead now, or almost. Natasha has already begun to fade from memory. If it wasn't for those scattered old photos, which could just as easily have been lost or destroyed, who would remember her face besides Vera and Jean? I'm torn: part of me wants to put the whole thing to bed, the other isn't quite ready to consign my mother to oblivion.

Meanwhile, I've inherited the recollection of a turquoise dress and the location of a gravestone. In a sense, that's more than I've had to go on for the last thirty-five years. But it's not much of a memory bank to draw from in years to come.

Hélène
x

Dear Hélène,

Stéphane has told me that you are piecing together our parents' story, and I'm taking the liberty of writing to you directly.

I enclose a photo that Marie and I found this weekend at Interlaken, in the chalet. My father left it there, among his papers. I couldn't find the negative so I photographed it and enlarged it, and made a print for you.

Hélène, you are the spitting image of your mother. And since Stéphane looks very much like Papa, I initially had the impression that it wasn't them, but you two in the photo. You must admit it's easy to be mistaken!

I don't know what my brother, to whom I have also sent the photo, will think of it. Between ourselves, Papa's memory is a very sensitive subject over which we do not always agree.

Unlike Stéphane, I had a stormy relationship with my parents until the end. But this photo doesn't make me angry, nor does it hurt me: in a way I find it comforting to know that my father was sometimes alive during his lifetime. The last ten years have at least taught me to stop hating him, and to show a little indulgence towards those who were my family, despite everything.

Marie sends her regards.

My very best wishes,

Philippe Crüsten

12

He is standing, she is sitting. They are perfectly positioned; the dissymmetry does not create an imbalance. She sits upright in the chair with bamboo arms. She is wearing dainty strap shoes that reveal her insteps, a faint lattice of veins visible beneath her skin. Her legs are crossed, emphasising the elegant pleats of her long skirt, the scallop caressing her ankles. Her pale, short-sleeved, scoop-necked blouse exposes her delicate collarbone and bare forearms; on her right arm is a silver bracelet in the form of two intertwined serpents. Her head is tilted slightly to one side: her cheekbones more prominent than ever, the hollows of her cheeks shadowy, her lips pressed together in a Mona Lisa smile. Her mass of short, frizzy hair frames her face. Then there are her eyes, slightly narrowed, distilling her gaze, which can be read as calm, or determined, or expressing the quiet certainty of being loved. Or all three at the same time.

His left hand, wearing a wedding ring, rests on her shoulder. His long, pale fingers are lying flat and slightly spread, touching the fabric of her blouse, without possessiveness, without false modesty either. Probably in that instant, the heat of their skins is already burning through the light cotton barrier, the flimsiest of obstacles to their desire. His next movement will probably be to withdraw his hand and brush Natasha's neck with his fingertips, with the same delicious thrill that comes from stroking an animal's fur. He too stares straight ahead. No averting his eyes, no frown, no irony. He is very much present in the photograph, present in the moment, present in the world, which amounts, in this instant, to the woman sitting a few centimetres from him. The intense expression in his strikingly pale eyes, the tiny wrinkles visible in the corners should be reinterpreted in the light of the total exultation that has taken possession of his body.

To anyone who didn't know these two people, they could be the embodiment of the trust that comes with love or marital bliss. They have stopped time, concentrated it entirely in the contact between a hand and a shoulder. They have accepted the promise of togetherness. Their beauties are not mutually exclusive but combine: the viewer's gaze follows the lines of two bodies that are calling to each other, melting into each other, fusing, like those of a painted portrait. In the tranquil eternity of the Jungfrau, which has unveiled in their honour the lacy outline of its ridges and the candour of its summer snows, Nataliya and Pierre have given to posterity the memory of a perfect moment, their moment: when two mortal bodies are sloughed off in the acceptance of finally becoming one.

Dear Stéphane,

I don't suppose I'll ever manage to commit another slip as blatantly Freudian as leaving the translation behind in Paris. I'd rather tell myself it was the right thing to do, because it allowed us to enjoy four days of total bliss together after too much time apart.

Back to reality: here is the scan. I have to admit I haven't yet read the original.

I think of you all the time and I can't wait for you to come to Paris. You won't have to sleep at Le Jardin Secret this time, as long as you don't mind being woken up at the crack of dawn by a hungry mog. If not perhaps even earlier by its owner.

Hélène
xxx

Diary of Jean Pamiat (1972–1973)

14 October

Natasha is pregnant by Pierre. She told her husband. He worked out the dates and realised immediately that the child could not be his. They argued, he hit her and threw her out of the house, saying he never wanted to see her again. She didn't even get the chance to kiss her daughter goodbye. She turned up here yesterday night, in shock and without any luggage, after a full day's travelling. The worst of it is that Pierre hasn't taken things any better; she called him at the studio to tell him and he put the phone down on her. She tried to call back but he wouldn't answer. She sent him a telegram to let him know that she was on her way and would be arriving by train and staying here, but he didn't show up. I am flabbergasted [he says he is angry but can't bring himself to believe it: *Boris*] by his reaction. Tomorrow, we are going to the studio, and I hope he will at least agree to speak to her. In the meantime, I shall try to get her to eat something and sleep a little.

15 October

The visit to the studio was a disaster. I stayed on the doorstep while they argued. After five minutes, Pierre started shouting things like 'It's out of the question! How could you?' Then they lowered their voices and I couldn't hear what they were saying. But when Natasha came back out, she was ashen. In the car, she told me he was scared to death, and terrified of Anna finding out. He won't hear a word about a divorce and wants her to go back to her husband. As she spoke, her voice was filled with bitterness. I've never seen her so dejected [very sad]. She looks ten years older than she did in the summer at Interlaken, yet it was barely a few weeks ago.

16 October

I went to the studio to try to see Pierre again, but he wouldn't let me in. I know he was in there; I could hear him moving around inside. I slipped a long letter under the door that Natasha wrote last night. The question is, will he read it?

24 October

Michel Hivert has given formal notice of his wife's desertion of the marital home and is asking for a divorce. The letter arrived here this morning; Natasha had given my address to Sylvia Makhno, who forwarded it. She's beside herself at the thought of her parents finding out and wants to keep the whole situation from them. 'It would kill them,' she said. It's true, I can't see Dr Zabvine taking a particularly philosophical view of things, let alone Daria, who spent every spare moment at Saint-Serge when they lived nearby. Still no news from Pierre.

26 October

I went with Natasha to see the lawyer, Maître Niemetz; she is desperate to see Lena at all costs. He is not very hopeful. He said that considering the circumstances and the fact Natasha has moved out, her husband will certainly be awarded custody of the little girl and she will have to be very patient to have any chance of seeing her. Nevertheless, he has written Michel Hivert a letter proposing a reconciliation [conciliation?] and a return to the marital home. Natasha said nothing while we were in there, but as soon as we left the office, she had an asthma attack which lasted over half an hour. She came home and went straight to sleep (I think she's taking Veronal [? = ВероНап ?])

She's stopped eating, hasn't had dinner all week. She says it's down to the morning sickness, but I think it's because she's given up hope. Pierre called this evening while she was asleep. He didn't want to speak to her. All he said was, 'Tell her I can't.' Can't what? Take responsibility? Leave his children? Clash with the

Krüger clan? When I hung up, I was filled with sadness at the thought of the message of betrayal he was asking me to deliver.

7 November

Michel Hivert has turned down the request for a reconciliation. It is now twenty-five days since Natasha last saw Lena. When I asked her yesterday what she was going to do, she replied flatly, 'Croak [die like an animal]. That would be best for everyone, wouldn't it?' I don't know what else I can do. I rummaged around in her bag while she was asleep and confiscated the Veronal.

9 November

Yesterday I took Natasha to see Séverine Crüsten in Besançon. I couldn't think who else to turn to. She took us into her kitchen and made us a coffee, even though it was late. Nataliya broke down and told her everything. When she had heard the whole story, Séverine flew into a rage. I don't think it was us she was angry with (I think she had guessed some time ago that Tasha and her son had begun seeing one another again and secretly approved), but Pierre, for letting down a woman who was carrying his child and had been thrown out of her home. She left the room to call his number in Geneva at midnight; I don't know what they said to one another but it quickly turned into an argument. 'Peter hung up on me,' Séverine announced when she came back downstairs. Then she asked me to leave the room, so that she could speak to Natasha in private. Their conversation went on for much of the night.

We met again at breakfast this morning. Natasha was red-eyed, but she seemed calmer. Though Séverine can be rather brusque, she treats Natasha with great kindness, like the sick little kittens she takes in from the wild; she has always been very fond of her. After we had eaten, she left us on our own, saying she had things to do. Natasha told me the gist of what they had talked about. Séverine asked if she wanted to keep the child. She said she would be there for Natasha whatever she decided to do, but she had to make up her mind quickly.

Poor Natasha ... she doesn't know which way to turn. In her heart, I think she would like to keep the baby. She's completely besotted with Pierre and it would be her dream to raise a son or daughter who looked like him. But she's afraid: jobless, facing a divorce, scared of hurting her parents ... Pierre's rejection hasn't exactly helped matters: she's realistic about the fact he won't be coming to her aid. But what scares her most, what keeps her awake at night, is the idea of never seeing Hélène again. So she's hoping that, just maybe, if she leaves Pierre and goes back to her husband, telling him she's miscarried, he will take her back to live with them again. Poor thing, she shouldn't be overly optimistic, if you ask me. He's Catholic, narrow-minded, and he'd no doubt rather make himself unhappy than give her a second chance. But the alternative for Natasha is unthinkable. She keeps asking, 'What about Lena? What's going to happen to Lena?' and then sinking into one of her endless silences. I think I'd go mad if I were her.

When Séverine came back, we agreed I would go to Geneva for one last attempt at getting Pierre to see sense, and that I would ring to let them know how I fared. Meanwhile, Natasha is to remain in Besançon. As I was leaving, Séverine whispered to me on the doorstep that she had been to see 'an old friend' and to make some calls from the phone box of a neighbouring village. She's being very careful, just in case. She has found a clinic in Lausanne, expensive at such short notice, but doesn't have enough cash to pay for it. On top of that, Natasha hasn't a *sou* in her pocket and no means of getting her savings book back.

I told S. not to worry, that I would bring the money back with me and we would pay whatever we had to. 'You must think me a monster,' she said wearily. Though her eyes had seen many things in their time, they were brimming with sadness. I think she would dearly love Tasha to have this baby, her grandson or granddaughter, and she couldn't care less about keeping up appearances or paying attention to gossip [other people's opinions]; her whole life, she has never given two hoots what people think of her. But she's under no illusions: she knows society at large won't be half as tolerant. May

'68 or not, Natasha remains a pregnant divorcee in their eyes. What's more, Séverine fears what it would do to her sanity were she to be prevented from seeing her young daughter again. As for me, there's nothing I can do, other than try to stop Natasha dying from an infection [сепсис], which is a distinct possibility if she has a back-street abortion. I shouldn't be writing all this in here, it's too risky. But everything is so hard at the moment, I feel the need to get it off my chest, if only to a diary. I hope writing in Russian will protect it from prying eyes.

11 November

I finally managed to speak to Pierre. He gave in and opened the door to end the racket I was making on his doorstep. He doesn't look too good himself: his hair's a mess, he hasn't shaved and there are dark circles under his eyes. It seems he has been sleeping at the studio recently. He told me he can't face seeing Natasha; that he loves her but there's nothing he can do, what with Anna and the children. He feels trapped and he won't leave. I tried to get across to him that the situation is much worse for Natasha; she has nothing left – no home, no money, no prospect even of seeing Lena – but he kept saying, 'I can't, I can't …' When I told him Natasha was considering an abortion, he made no comment.

For him to simply give up on Natasha, when he loves her with all his heart, is just too painful to watch. I know full well that his wife has never been more than second-best. Yet he must also be afraid of losing his boys and his reputation in Geneva. Of course, to go against his all-powerful in-laws would be tough, but how will he be able to face himself in the mirror after this? How can he go on playing happy families with his wife and kids? Whether he wants the child or not, he can't turn his back on Nataliya like this, not now. I tried to make him see that if he lets her down, he'll regret it for the rest of his life, but he sat by the window, turned away and didn't say another word.

12 November

I couldn't face making the phone call so I got in the car and drove straight back to Besançon. I spent the whole journey trying to work out how I was going to tell Natasha, but when I arrived, she was already asleep. Séverine says her spirits are sinking even lower. She only goes out for a few hours each day to take a walk to the little chapel, sometimes in our company, sometimes alone.

Though the mild autumn days have abruptly given way to winter, we went out onto the terrace to smoke after dinner. Séverine, normally bounding with energy, looked tired. She said something to me – or to herself, perhaps.

'You see, Jean, you give birth to your children, you do everything you can for them. You try to give them courage, you have faith in them. But at the end of the day, you look at these men you've tried to mould into decent human beings and you realise they're exactly the same as us. Always coming up with a million excuses for not facing up to the chaos they've created.'

I watched the smoke coming out of her nostrils, two little spirals curling upwards in the cold air. I thought how strange the situation was – the mother, the mistress and the best friend – and I pictured Pierre drifting away from us, as if an impostor had taken the place of the man we all knew. A few metres away inside the house, a tiny spark of life was flickering in Natasha's belly: would we be its fairy godparents or its Fates? I said to Séverine that Pierre must be terrified, that he probably needed time for everything to sink in.

'Time is what we're all lacking, my dear,' she replied, stubbing out her cigarette in the ashtray in one swift movement.

13 November

I spoke to Natasha this morning. She took everything in without saying a word. But for a brief moment, the shock and pain froze her face. She has finally decided to have an abortion. Séverine made some more calls and got her an appointment in four days' time. We've managed to scrape together enough cash. Everything should be fine. I will drive her to Lausanne. Now that the decision has been made, we're all feeling relieved. I called the paper and told them I was ill and wouldn't be back at work until Saturday. Luckily, Kreyder owed me a favour and has agreed to cover my most pressing assignments.

I can't wait for all of this to be over. It's not easy seeing Natasha in this state. I don't know what to make of Pierre's reaction: part of me understands his fear, but I can't condone the appalling way in which he has shirked his responsibilities. I used to think he was an artist who had stumbled into a world that was not his own; now he's acting like a true bourgeois living in fear of scandal. And yet this is the man who ended up with two broken ribs and a split eyebrow, protecting me when some idiots from our battalion in Castelnaudry got hold of an iron bar and decided it was time for a bit of queer bashing [he uses coarser language]. Where on earth did that courage go? I sometimes find myself wishing none of this had ever happened, that life could go back to the way it was before, back to the summer of 1970 in Interlaken. But those carefree days will never return.

17 November

Terrible migraine last night. Couldn't stop throwing up. Passed out. Morphine. Had to let Natasha go on her own. Waiting for the call.

18 November

1 a.m. No news. Natasha never reached the clinic.

I should not have let her go alone, but what was I supposed to do? Sent a telegram to Pierre who replied by same means to say she is not in Geneva. Séverine went to the post office this afternoon to look up the husband's number. She called, but a woman answered (a housekeeper?) and told her he no longer lives there. I have an awful feeling about this. We're hoping Natasha just changed her mind and stopped at a hotel somewhere. But why doesn't she call?

2 p.m. Had a phone call from Pontarlier hospital earlier asking if we knew a Nataliya Zabvina. They had found her purse with her identity card and Séverine's number inside. They won't say anything else, just asked us to come at once. We're at the station; train is about to arrive.

19 November

Natasha is dead.

24 November

Funeral. Couldn't get hold of her husband in time. He's on manoeuvres somewhere and all the French police could do was pass the message to his high command. Given the state of the roads – at least a metre of snow has fallen in the last two days and the main road is blocked – nobody was prepared to transport the body to Paris. So, after four days, we had to resign ourselves to having Nataliya buried at Pontarlier cemetery. I had called the Zabvines from the hospital and they arrived the following day. They're devastated. Sylvia brought them here; she has barely said a word. When I put my arms around her, she started crying soundlessly. Pierre was there too – what's left of him, at least. He stood very straight, numb, his mother white-faced by his side.

We are all living a nightmare now.

29 December

A month has passed since Natasha's death and still I keep expecting her to walk through the door at any moment. I haven't felt up to writing this diary since the funeral – too hard. I don't know when I'll be able to sleep through the night again.

When she set off for Lausanne that morning, heading for the clinic where she would undergo an illegal abortion, I couldn't go with her because I was laid low with a migraine. I couldn't stop throwing up. A local doctor came to give me a morphine injection and I passed out. It's ridiculous to abandon someone in their hour of need because of a headache, yet that's exactly what happened. Séverine was thinking of going in my stead, but her rather too frequent 'travels' meant she had been grilled at the border more than once before, and her eyesight was no longer good enough to drive back. Since Natasha had her passport with her, but not her driving licence, which she had left in Brest, she had to avoid attracting attention at all costs. Séverine tried to get hold of another of her 'old friends' to ask him to stand in, but he wasn't at home. Calling on mere acquaintances was too risky; there was always the chance of being reported. Neither could we postpone the appointment we had paid a fortune to secure.

So Natasha got behind the wheel of my Peugeot alone. I can vaguely remember her coming in to say goodbye before she left. I didn't want her to hug me; I was covered in sweat. So instead she stroked my forehead. It was a strange, slightly maternal gesture, and stands out in my memory because we didn't normally touch. I can still recall the feel of her hand, so cool against my tender skin. She said something in Russian: that everything would be fine, I think.

We had agreed she would call us when she arrived and I would take the first train to join her the following day. Séverine told me later she had had a coffee before she left and had seemed in good spirits, knowing her ordeal was almost over. She wanted to repay Séverine for her hospitality, when she could, but Séverine wouldn't hear of it. She kissed her and told her to take care of herself.

'For the first time since she got here,' Séverine said, 'she seemed calm, determined, clear-sighted. I wasn't worried.'

The car came off the road somewhere between Pontarlier and La Cluse and fell into a fairly deep ravine. According to the gendarmes, the road had been icy and it was snowing. Since there were no skid marks, their theory was she didn't see the bend in the road and ploughed straight through the safety barrier at full speed.

She didn't die instantly, but was taken to hospital in Pontarlier. She was in a coma when we arrived. Her chest had been crushed and she had sustained a head injury. The doctors gave us no hope, and she died at dawn from cerebral oedema. All night long I held her lifeless hand, the same soft hand that had stroked my face just hours before. Tasha was unrecognisable: her face was swollen, her head had been shaved and bandaged, and there were tubes and drips sticking out of her. Just before she died, she opened her eyes and stared at me with an intensity I had never seen in a human gaze. Her neurologist thinks it was a reflex, but I believe she gathered up all the life left in her to try to pass on one last message, which she never managed to convey.

I don't remember what kind of state I was in. I can't have eaten or slept for over twenty-four hours. The doctor, who took me to be her husband, pronounced her dead almost in a whisper. He got me to sign a register and gave me Natasha's bag, which still held the money sealed inside a brown envelope. It was a hard-sided, boxy, ugly leather bag which didn't suit her; she must have bought it with the money I lent her. It hit home that she had died miles away from her daughter, her parents, her books, without the slightest familiar object beside her. The bile rose in my throat and I gagged. As for Séverine, she sat in the waiting room chain-smoking, saying nothing, staring at the peeling paintwork.

Back out in the open in the hospital car park, there was that strange atmosphere that comes before snow. I remember clearly the damp, heavy smell, the feeling of the cool air against my face, the incongruous memory of an afternoon's skiing surfacing. And it struck me like a knife in the stomach that everything was over. I think that's when it sank in. I started crying like a baby in Séverine's arms, oblivious to the stares of all around us.

We walked until we found a taxi willing to take us to Geneva despite the forecast. Driving conditions were appalling and we didn't speak for the entire journey. When we reached the top of the steps leading up to the studio, we stood there for at least five minutes before one of us (Séverine, I think) found the courage to knock. Pierre looked surprised and a little disappointed to see us.

'Maman, what are you doing here?' Neither of us replied. 'Did Natasha get my letter?'

It's all a bit of a blur, but somehow at that moment all the pain, lack of sleep, shock and migraine came together and I started hitting Pierre like a madman [he literally says 'hitting like a demon']. I think I wanted to kill him. I called him every name under the sun, shouting at him in Russian and screaming that Natasha was dead. He couldn't understand a word I was saying. Séverine had to step in and tell him herself.

Afterwards, there was a long silence. Pierre had a faraway look in his eyes, as though his mind was elsewhere. I don't think he had taken in the meaning of what Séverine had just said. Just then, I heard the sound of a record playing from the floor above. It was one of those syrupy [sugary] ballads by Zarah Leander, 'Sag' mir nicht Adieu, sag' nur auf Wiedersehen'. For one awful moment the three of us stood listening to that ghastly refrain, and then Pierre sank ever so slowly to the floor, as if his muscles could no longer support him. His eyes glazed over; he was drained, utterly drained. The song ended, silence fell and it held us there, frozen. In a sense, it has still not let go of us.

What followed was like a nightmare without end: going to wait for the Zabvines, and Sylvia, who was driving them (I had sent her a telegram); our failure to reach the husband. The three of us headed back to Pontarlier in spite of the blizzard that had begun to swirl. Pierre didn't speak, not a word. He only cracked when faced with the body at the morgue; on top of everything else, our beautiful Natasha had been subjected to an autopsy. When he left the room, I could see that the image of her on the slab had been imprinted on his retina, on his very being, and would haunt him for the rest of his life. His legs moved, his body functioned, but inside, he was a dead man.

Having endured the coroner, Séverine and I were treated to a barrage of questions from the police [cops].

Their tone was suspicious and needling, because they had realised the reason for Natasha's journey. They said she must have been on something, or else it was suicide, and they made us answer dozens of questions about her – and ourselves, too. Séverine stood her ground and eventually they let us go.

We couldn't find an Orthodox priest so Natasha was buried in a Catholic ceremony. What I remember most was the biting wind and how horrible it was to have to leave her there in the cold. Daria was sobbing, Oleg stood stock still. Just once he looked up at Pierre, whom he had recognised, and from the look in his eyes I could tell that he, one of the gentlest people you could hope to meet, would have liked to strangle the man with his bare hands. He's no fool: he knew very well that his thirty-one-year-old daughter wasn't there being covered in earth in deepest Jura simply because she had skidded off a bend in the road. After the ceremony, I took the Zabvines for a steaming hot cup of tea in a café that reeked of cabbage and burnt fat. We were numb with cold. We spoke in Russian. Stiff as a waxwork, Oleg kept saying, 'We must tell Michel. We must tell Michel,' while Daria wrung her hands and wondered what would become of Lena – just as Natasha had done a few days earlier. My heart bleeds when I think of that little girl who does not yet know that her mother is dead and that she will never see her again.

31 December

After the funeral, Sylvia left the car behind and took the train back with the Zabvines, who were a pitiful sight; their grief seemed to have aged them several years. I drove Pierre back to Geneva in his car, taking the wheel myself for fear he might do something stupid. The road was icy, it was snowing, I skidded several times, and I thought how Natasha must have felt the moment she crashed through the barrier.

We will never know whether or not it was deliberate. She loved life, better and more fully than anyone else I know, but life had quietly sapped her before letting her down completely, betraying her. She knew she had lost everything: her daughter, her unborn child, her husband and the man she loved. Had she decided to end the suffering that seemed to pursue her at every turn? She leaves the question behind her; the answer died with her. Now it's our turn to suffer.

Here, the New Year festivities are in full swing, which only makes everything feel all the more poignant. I haven't seen Pierre, Séverine or the Zabvines for a month and a half. I don't know when or how Michel Hivert heard the news, or whether he has been able to visit his wife's grave. Yesterday I got the letter Pierre had sent Natasha, returned to me from Besançon; in the note she sent with it, Séverine told me it arrived two days after the accident. She said she would rather

I return it to her son. But I don't think I will. Whatever he might have written in it, it was too late.

1 January

Tried to develop the photos, but didn't get beyond the first contact sheet. I feel terrible that all I have to send the Zabvines is one blurry picture, when they're yearning for something to cling on to. But I was shaking too much that day. And not because of the cold. When I came out of the darkroom, I drank myself into a stupor.

2 January

Today I packed up all Natasha's things – her jewellery, the contents of her bag – and sent them to her husband. I feel sorry for him. He's not a bad man. He was always off with a book or away somewhere with the army, and the fact of the matter is that Natasha only married him to please her father. I don't think she ever felt anything more than fondness for him. And that fondness wasn't enough to hold her back when her path crossed Pierre's again, two years ago. Now, the husband has become a widower, and has to live with the fact that the last time he saw his wife was when he threw her out. I wouldn't like to be in his shoes. But I don't much like being in mine either.

13 February

Received a note from Oleg Zabvine saying Michel Hivert has flatly refused to see him and Daria. They fear they will never see Lena again and are utterly distraught.

15 June

I've been trying to find out where Lena is for the past two months, but Michel Hivert has moved house without leaving a forwarding address. Needless to say, his parents are covering for him and claim to know nothing. The Zabvines managed to have Natasha's body brought back to Thiais. They go and visit her there every Sunday.

17 September

Daria Zabvina, née Golytsina,

regrets to inform you of the death of her husband,

Dr Oleg Zabvine,

who passed away in Paris, aged 64.

The funeral will be held in Paris at l'Église Saint-Serge (19th *arrondissement*)

on 14 September 1973 at 3 p.m.

---

18 November

It will be a year tomorrow. It feels like yesterday. I can't get the images out of my mind; I see Natasha in almost every nightmare. Old Dr Zabvine died of a broken heart.

22 November

Yesterday I put Pierre's letter in an envelope and wrote 'For Lena' on it. I sent it to Sylvia Makhno with instructions to pass it on when the time comes. She is the little girl's godmother and, with luck, Hivert will come round eventually and let her and Daria see her. It seems to me that the child is the only possible person to whom these words – whatever they may be – can now be conveyed, words which no longer have currency for us. She will grow up and one day seek the truth – that's for certain. She will want to know what killed her mother. And we may no longer be around to provide the answer.

We have been bystanders to something bigger than all of us. Ten years of separation, marriage, children, none of it made the slightest difference: they still loved one another. You only had to look at them, the way they stood so close to one another even without touching. Natasha once told me that all the time they had spent apart had been like living in a coma. Once they had found one another again, they might as well have tried to hold back the ocean. They didn't even put up a fight.

Who, then, is to blame? They are, of course, for having given in to it, instead of going back to their respective lives and putting it all behind them. The Zabvines, for forcing Natasha to break off the engagement back in 1960 because they didn't want their daughter marrying a penniless photographer. Michel Hivert, for leaving Natasha to raise their daughter alone, oblivious to the fact he was losing her. Sylvia, for refusing to listen when Natasha needed her most. Séverine, for setting up the appointment at that clinic. Me, for letting her take the wheel alone. And Pierre – Pierre, who, for all that he was madly in love with her, could never quite make up his mind, when she would have sacrificed everything for him. He thought the odd summer in Interlaken and a few snatched days in Brittany were all he had to offer, and spent his life hoping some miraculous solution to all his problems would suddenly materialise. Perhaps the truth is he never quite forgave her for breaking off their engagement and had resolved to sacrifice nothing for the woman who had given him up.

Once the wheels were in motion, was there ever a chance to stop them turning? Which of us missed our chance to put a spoke in and prevent the inevitable tragedy? I can't stop these thoughts from going round in my head at night. I remember mentioning offhand that I was due to meet Natasha in Dinard with the Vassilyevs, and Pierre begging me to bring back a photograph of her. Would he have forgotten her had I not obeyed? Although she was pregnant at the time, I could tell from the way he ran his finger over the image that the sight of her had lifted some hidden barrier inside him, reactivating a virus that had lain dormant. Then the tragic train of events rolled onwards. Pierre turned up unannounced in Interlaken in 1970, finding us at the chalet to which Natasha had fled to have a break from her suffocating marriage. The look, my God, the look they gave one another, both stopping to touch their engagement rings at exactly the same time, as total silence descended on the room … A moment later, Pierre had wrapped his arms slowly, painfully around her. He embraced her so gently, the way you would hold a bundle of delicate twigs [small branches], and her entire body let itself be enveloped, dissolving into the calm passion that whispered from one atom of flesh to another: love me, love me, love me again.

I spent the night elsewhere. The next morning, I found them sitting side by side on the sofa, still entwined in their sleep, both fully dressed. Natasha's head rested against Pierre's neck. There was a look of peace on their faces, as if they had safely returned to port after a crossing fraught with dangers. I don't think they had even made love. And even though I knew the affair would wreak havoc on the lives of all involved, I said to myself I would give anything to feel so totally attuned to another person.

20 December

Difficult to write in this diary. When I started it, Nataliya was still alive. Now both she and Oleg are dead, and her husband has vanished into thin air, taking Lena with him.

I've been seeing quite a bit of Pierre. He's a shadow of his former self. He has never told me what he wrote to Natasha; whether he had a last-minute change of heart. The few times I have tried to mention her have met with stony silence. His marriage is a sham, but he's staying for the sake of the children. To begin with, I thought he was going to kill himself. He wasn't eating properly and was drinking heavily; he came close to losing the studio. And then, little by little, life, photos, albums took hold once more. But he barely speaks, and when he does it's in monosyllables. His poor children can't make sense of it, and Anna has become worryingly bigoted in her opinions. I visit once a fortnight and try to get the boys out of this poisonous [bad] atmosphere. This tragedy has already caused so much harm, and they are still so innocent.

25 December

Spent Christmas Day with the Crüstens. Mood was glum. Nevertheless, Anna and Pierre did their best to avoid spoiling the children's day. I bought a new racquet for Philippe and an illustrated encyclopedia of plants for Stéphane, who has become fascinated by trees. The boys came out to the car to say goodbye and, after I had hugged each of them, my godson whispered in my ear: 'Jean, why doesn't Papa love us any more?'

He's only little, Stéphane, but he's already very solemn and earnest, with his big blue eyes and blond curls tumbling onto his forehead. It's clear he is taking things badly, because he doesn't understand what's going on.

I placed my hand on his neck, bent down to look him straight in the eyes and told him, 'He does love you, I promise. He's just very sad at the moment.'

Stéphane bit his lip and thought for a moment before asking, 'When will he stop being sad?'

I gave him the only reply that seemed honest: as soon as he can.

And I told him to try not to think about it.

Dearest Hélène,

I have just finished reading Jean's diary. That certainly puts a new slant on things. It really is a never-ending web of lies.

I confess I'm feeling at a loss. When I awoke beside you in Saint-Malo, you were still asleep, and I watched you for a long time. At that point, I no longer believed that this search would really shed any light on the past, but I didn't care. It had given me that moment of perfect happiness. That gift of fate was a miracle in itself.

After reading Sylvia's letter (she apparently knew nothing of your mother's final days), I was even more convinced that the past had finished unloading its toxic burden. As far as I was concerned, Nataliya had died in a car crash on her way to meet my father, when they were both probably on the point of divorcing. Nothing less, but nothing more.

Jean's diary changes everything: an irresponsible coward, a reckless, suicidal woman, our dear parents seem a little less endearing this evening. Not to mention the others, only too eager to hush the whole thing up, I suppose, so as not to have to face up to their own part in this disaster.

All of a sudden I feel as if I've inherited a heap of failures, defeats and disgraces of which I was oblivious. I wonder what you will think of me, the son of the man who drove your mother to despair, and in a way to her grave. How will I be able to forget that you are the daughter of the woman whose death spelled the destruction of our family? I wonder to what extent we aren't the subjects of a cruel game, the panic-stricken negative of the couple that half gave birth to us both. And whether we will be able to avoid treading in their footsteps and repeating their mistakes.

These are not ghosts we have exhumed: they are very much alive; it is as if they will never stop spreading sorrow around them. I really do believe I hate them. And one of the reasons for this hatred is that their affair weighs heavily on ours, to the point of suffocation, and I'm terrified at the idea of losing you. So I picked up my pen, as in the early days of our correspondence, in the hope that the evil spell will have been warded off, I don't know how, by the time these words reach you.

Show me the way.

Stéphane

Paris, 2 April 2008

Stéphane,

You feel totally adrift, I know, and with good reason. But don't judge them, let's not judge them.

While you've been wallowing in resentment, I've spent the last few evenings walking beside Canal Saint-Martin, thinking of them. I kept walking until I had run through every question in my mind and vented all the anger, outrage, sometimes fury I had for all of them – our parents, Sylvia and Michel. Finally I came round to hating myself, for having opened Pandora's box.

And then I calmed down.

Because I realised there was really very little standing between them and us. We are looking upon them as two parents with a debt to pay, and we're summoning them to be tried posthumously before us. We loathe them for not having been there for us, for keeping things from us, for their adultery and lies. But at the end of the day, they were just themselves: a man and a woman in love, torn between the feelings they had for one another and for their families.

All their efforts to deny that passion, all the pressure they put themselves under only made matters worse. A broken engagement, two marriages, children and distance could not put an end to it. The fact that they were reunited proves that the bond between them had withstood all the obstacles life – or they themselves – had thrown in their way.

We are looking down at their lives from the vantage point of the world today, with our freedoms already won. It's easy. But my mother was a minor until the age of twenty-one and was married at twenty-seven: she spent almost her entire life in a state of subjection, first to her family and then to her husband. Yes, she fell pregnant by your father. Perhaps they could have avoided it, perhaps not: it wasn't half as easy to get hold of the pill in the 1970s.

By going for an abortion, she was taking a huge risk; private clinic or no clinic, there's no knowing what the consequences would have been. Yet she was willing to go down that road because she would have done anything, including losing the child of the man she loved, to see me again. I could never hold that against her. I could never blame her for having been scared. At the risk of shocking you, I'm even less minded to blame her given that I too was once on the brink of making that decision, and it cost me a ten-year relationship (the famous Hervé whom Sylvia referred to). That's when I realised that some obstacles simply cannot be overcome and we will do anything to get around them, even if it destroys us. And I'm convinced that if my mother chose this desperate option, it's because she felt trapped and could see no other way out. Indeed, Jean's entire diary tells us it was so.

No, your father's behaviour doesn't exactly cover him in glory, but to conclude that his silence was what pushed my mother into the ravine is absurd, just as absurd as the idea she threw herself over the edge on purpose. Pierre was scared. Most of all, I suspect, of losing his children. I know you've said he wasn't around much; but you all knew who he was, what he was doing, where to find him. Philippe told me your father stood by your mother all the way through her illness: it's not often you come across such loyalty through trials and discord, and that loyalty is doubtless the clearest sign he was not totally without integrity. With my mother, Pierre never had the chance to make up for his mistakes; the accident froze him in the role of bastard for posterity.

Every single day after Nataliya's death must have been a living hell for all of them. How often must he and Michel Hivert have blamed themselves? Do you imagine they were able, just for one day, for one night, to forget that they had both rejected the woman they loved and had lost her for ever? When it seemed to us we were falling foul of their bad moods, what you and I were really seeing was the guilt gnawing away at them, their every memory a torment. Thirty years on, your father was still visiting Natasha's grave, and mine was still slamming doors every time he heard Sylvia call me Lena. Don't be too hard on them, Stéphane. In life, it seems to me they were hard enough on themselves.

My feeling is that it's time to forgive what they and those around them never forgave themselves for. Pierre and Nataliya loved one another, they loved us and, whether we like it or not, we are the heirs to that love. Those left behind kept their lips sealed, but they did so in order to protect themselves and to protect us. They don't deserve our censure either.

There's no denying we have suffered. And we have not yet fully unravelled the harsh truth which has already brought such pain, filling your father's 220 albums with such indelible sadness. But the conclusion you came to in an earlier letter is the right one. We are now the sole beneficiaries of this past, so we alone are responsible for deciding what to do with it.

When I think of the two of them now, Stéphane, I marvel at the strength of their bond, the same bond that brought us together thirty-seven years later from the unlikely beginnings of a newspaper clipping. The way we felt sipping our first coffee together that sunny morning in Saint-Malo, the low February light rippling on the sea like glass and gold leaf — it's them we have to thank for it. Yes, it was the people in the photo speaking to us, calling our names … I gaze into their faces until my head spins and I seem to hear them telling us it's time to live, to seize the opportunity they let slip away.

I want nothing more than for you to come back to me.

And for us to love one another.

Hélène

xxxx

These are two photos that no one will ever see. One, horrifying, of a Peugeot 504 that has come off the road and plunged into a ravine. The barrier smashed and gaping, a heap of mangled metal, wheels in the air, shrubs torn up as the car hurtled down, brown gashes in the earth mingled with the snow giving this grisly scene an incongruous, melancholy beauty. The image lies in a police file, stored with others in a box, piled up in a warehouse containing thousands of similar boxes. After the prescribed length of time, when the continuous arrival of new files, archives and forensic evidence will make it necessary to free up the space, the box will be loaded onto a pallet, then transferred to a dump truck whose content will be emptied into an incinerator, where it will end its journey.

Meanwhile, as the police photographer is clicking the shutter, a tormented man in a cluttered room in Geneva is looking at himself in the mirror. His face is haggard, with dark rings around his eyes. He hasn't shaved for three days. His shirt looks somewhat the worse for wear. However, the anguish that had compressed the blue of his gaze around a dark slit, like a cat's elliptical pupils, has dispelled. It has given way to the weary certainty that comes from surrender after a long battle, to the relaxation that comes with relief. And the man, who has not touched a camera for three weeks, decides right then that he is going to try and photograph this winter moment.

Soon the spring will be back, and the heat of the sun's rays will come and caress the skin of his model to whom he has the previous day written a decisive letter for their joint future. He envisages sitting her not far from the window, on a white stool, her silhouette accentuating the small bump of a swelling belly. Before returning to the camera, he will place his hands on her slender forearms and the bracelet with two serpents and let them rest there for a few seconds, his eyes looking deep into those of the young woman, like a farewell before crossing over to the far shore of the gaze. And on that day he knows he will take the definitive photo, the alpha and omega of all the sights the world has given him. He will succeed in forcing matter, impermanence, death, oblivion to surrender. The lights, conquered by his ultimate gesture, slaves of the mechanical spell, will converge on the face of one single woman, to write in the image a truth ordinarily destined to escape it: love, once born, whatever the fate reserved for it, is irreversible.